Boyhood Dreams and Other Tales

Ruskin Bond is known for his signature simplistic and witty writing style. He is the author of several bestselling short stories, novellas, collections, essays and children's books; and has contributed a number of poems and articles to various magazines and anthologies. At the age of twenty-three, he won the prestigious John Llewellyn Rhys Prize for his first novel, *The Room on the Roof*. He was also the recipient of the Padma Shri in 1999, Lifetime Achievement Award by the Delhi Government in 2012, and the Padma Bhushan in 2014.

Born in 1934, Ruskin Bond grew up in Jamnagar, Shimla, New Delhi and Dehradun. Apart from three years in the UK, he has spent all his life in India, and now lives in Landour, Mussoorie, with his adopted family.

RUSKIN BOND

Boyhood Dreams and Other Tales

RUPA

Published by
Rupa Publications India Pvt. Ltd 2019
161-B/4, Gulmohar House,
Yusuf Sarai Community Centre,
New Delhi 110049

Sales centres:
Bengaluru Chennai
Hyderabad Kolkata Mumbai

This is a work of fiction. Names, characters, places and incidents are either the product of the author's imagination or are used fictitiously and any resemblance to any actual person, living or dead, events or locales is entirely coincidental.

P-ISBN: 978-93-5333-670-7
E-ISBN: 978-93-5333-671-4

Sixth impression 2026

10 9 8 7 6

Printed in India

CONTENTS

INTRODUCTION

The beauty of short fiction is that, with only a few pages, it can leave a lasting impact on the reader.

Boyhood Dreams and Other Tales is a collection of several of my short stories written over half a century. This includes my popular children's novellas such as *The Blue Umbrella* and *A Long Walk for Bina* and an excerpt from my novel *The Room on the Roof.* Some tales of love that I've penned, like 'Time Stops at Shamli', 'The Eyes Have It' and 'Love Is a Sad Song', go back to my twenties and thirties. There are stories that came from nostalgia and memories, such as 'The Kitemaker'and 'From Small Beginnings'. I have also included a few animal stories in this collection—'The Monkeys', 'The Hare in the Moon' and 'The Tunnel'.

It is through these stories that I put down on paper the many characters in my head, the idiosyncratic folks I encounter, some odd dreams and old memories before they fade away... It is wonderful to have the freedom to write on anything that has taken one's fancy.

Life has its ups and downs and periods of darkness, but now and then you need a little cheer to uplift your mood and to keep you sailing. Fiction, I believe, is a great resort at such a time. I hope you, dear reader, will enjoy these stories of mine and that these characters that I've created will keep you enthralled at all times.

Ruskin Bond

THE KITEMAKER

There was but one tree in the street known as Gali Ram Nath—an ancient banyan that had grown through the cracks of an abandoned mosque—and little Ali's kite was caught in its branches. The boy, barefoot and clad only in a torn shirt, ran along the cobbled stones of the narrow street to where his grandfather sat nodding dreamily in the sunshine in their back courtyard.

'Grandfather,' shouted the boy. 'My kite has gone!'

The old man woke from his daydream with a start and, raising his head, displayed a beard that would have been white had it not been dyed red with mehendi leaves.

'Did the twine break?' he asked. 'I know that kite twine is not what it used to be.'

'No, Grandfather, the kite is stuck in the banyan tree.'

The old man chuckled. 'You have yet to learn how to fly a kite properly, my child. And I am too old to teach you, that's the pity of it. But you shall have another.'

He had just finished making a new kite from bamboo, paper and thin silk, and it lay in the sun, firming up. It was a pale pink kite, with a small green tail. The old man handed it to Ali, and the boy raised himself on his toes and kissed his grandfather's hollowed-out cheek.

'I will not lose this one,' he said. 'This kite will fly like a bird.' And he turned on his heels and skipped out of the courtyard.

The old man remained dreaming in the sun. His kite shop was gone, the premises long since sold to a junk dealer; but he still made kites, for his own amusement and for the benefit of his grandson, Ali. Not many people bought kites these days. Adults disdained them, and children preferred to spend their money at the cinema. Moreover, there were not many open spaces left for the flying of kites. The city had swallowed up the open grassland that had stretched from the old fort's walls to the river bank.

But the old man remembered a time when grown men flew kites, and great battles were fought, the kites swerving and swooping in the sky, tangling with each other until the string of one was severed. Then the defeated but liberated kite would float away into the blue unknown. There was a good deal of betting, and money frequently changed hands.

Kite flying was then the sport of kings, and the old man remembered how the Nawab himself would come down to the riverside with his retinue to participate in this noble pastime. There was time, then, to spend an idle hour with a gay, dancing strip of paper. Now everyone hurried, in a heat of hope, and delicate things like kites and daydreams were trampled underfoot.

He, Mehmood the kitemaker, had in the prime of his life been well known throughout the city. Some of his more elaborate kites once sold for as much as three or four rupees each.

At the request of the Nawab he had once made a very special kind of kite, unlike any that had been seen in the district. It consisted of a series of small, very light paper disks trailing on a thin bamboo frame. To the end of each disk he fixed a sprig of grass, forming a balance on both sides. The surface of the foremost disk was slightly convex, and a fantastic face was painted on it, having two eyes made of small mirrors. The disks, decreasing in size from head to tail, assumed an undulatory form and gave the kite the appearance of a crawling serpent. It required great skill to raise this cumbersome device from the ground, and only Mehmood could manage it.

Everyone had heard of the 'Dragon Kite' that Mehmood had

built, and word went round that it possessed supernatural powers. A large crowd assembled in the open to watch its first public launching in the presence of the Nawab.

At the first attempt it refused to leave the ground. The disks made a plaintive, protesting sound, and the sun was trapped in the little mirrors, making the kite a living, complaining creature. Then the wind came from the right direction, and the Dragon Kite soared into the sky, wriggling its way higher and higher, the sun still glinting in its devil eyes. And when it went very high, it pulled fiercely at the twine, and Mehmood's young sons had to help him with the reel. Still the kite pulled, determined to be free, to break loose, to live a life of its own. And eventually it did so.

The twine snapped, the kite leaped away towards the sun, sailing on heavenward until it was lost to view. It was never found again, and Mehmood wondered afterwards if he had made too vivid, too living a thing of the great kite. He did not make another like it. Instead he presented to the Nawab a musical kite, one that made a sound like a violin when it rose into the air.

Those were more leisurely, more spacious days. But the Nawab had died years ago, and his descendants were almost as poor as Mehmood himself. Kitemakers, like poets, once had their patrons; but now no one knew Mehmood, simply because there were too many people in the Gali, and they could not be bothered with their neighbours.

When Mehmood was younger and had fallen sick, everyone in the neighbourhood had come to ask after his health; but now, when his days were drawing to a close, no one visited him. Most of his old friends were dead and his sons had grown up: one was working in a local garage and the other, who was in Pakistan at the time of the Partition, had not been able to rejoin his relatives.

The children who had bought kites from him ten years ago were now grown men, struggling for a living; they did not have time for the old man and his memories. They had grown up in a swiftly changing and competitive world, and they looked at the old kitemaker and the banyan tree with the same indifference.

Both were taken for granted—permanent fixtures that were of no concern to the raucous, sweating mass of humanity that surrounded them. No longer did people gather under the banyan tree to discuss their problems and their plans; only in the summer months did a few seek shelter from the fierce sun.

But there was the boy, his grandson. It was good that Mehmood's son worked close by, for it gladdened the old man's heart to watch the small boy at play in the winter sunshine, growing under his eyes like a young and well-nourished sapling putting forth new leaves each day. There is a great affinity between trees and men. We grow at much the same pace, if we are not hurt or starved or cut down. In our youth we are resplendent creatures, and in our declining years we stoop a little, we remember, we stretch our brittle limbs in the sun, and then, with a sigh, we shed our last leaves.

Mehmood was like the banyan, his hands gnarled and twisted like the roots of the ancient tree. Ali was like the young mimosa planted at the end of the courtyard. In two years, both he and the tree would acquire the strength and confidence of their early youth.

The voices in the street grew fainter, and Mehmood wondered if he was going to fall asleep and dream, as he so often did, of a kite so beautiful and powerful that it would resemble the great white bird of the Hindus—Garuda, God Vishnu's famous steed. He would like to make a wonderful new kite for little Ali. He had nothing else to leave the boy.

He heard Ali's voice in the distance, but did not realize that the boy was calling him. The voice seemed to come from very far away.

Ali was at the courtyard door, asking if his mother had as yet returned from the bazaar. When Mehmood did not answer, the boy came forward repeating his question. The sunlight was slanting across the old man's head, and a small white butterfly rested on his flowing beard. Mehmood was silent; and when Ali put his small brown hand on the old man's shoulder, he met with no response. The boy heard a faint sound, like the rubbing of marbles in his pocket.

Suddenly afraid, Ali turned and moved to the door, and then ran down the street shouting for his mother. The butterfly left the old man's beard and flew to the mimosa tree, and a sudden gust of wind caught the torn kite and lifted it in the air, carrying it far above the struggling city into the blind blue sky.

TIME STOPS AT SHAMLI

The Dehra Express usually drew into Shamli at about five o'clock in the morning, at which time the station would be dimly lit and the jungle across the tracks would just be visible in the faint light of dawn. Shamli is a small station at the foot of the Siwalik hills, and the Siwaliks lie at the foot of the Himalayas, which in turn lie at the feet of God.

The station, I remember, had only one platform, an office for the station-master, and a waiting-room. The platform boasted a tea-stall, a fruit vendor, and a few stray dogs; not much else was required, because the train stopped at Shamli for only five minutes before rushing on into the forests.

Why it stopped at Shamli, I never could tell. Nobody got off the train and nobody got in. There were never any coolies on the platform. But the train would stand there a full five minutes, and the guard would blow his whistle, and presently Shamli would be left behind and forgotten...until I passed that way again...

I was paying my relations in Saharanpur an annual visit, when the night train stopped at Shamli. I was thirty-six at the time, and still single.

On this particular journey, the train came into Shamli just as I awoke from a restless sleep. The third class compartment was crowded beyond capacity, and I had been sleeping in an upright position, with my back to the lavatory door. Now someone was trying to get into the lavatory. He was obviously hardpressed for time.

'I'm sorry, brother,' I said, moving as much as I could do to one side.

He stumbled into the closet without bothering to close the door.

'Where are we now?' I asked the man sitting beside me. He was smoking a strong aromatic bidi.

'Shamli station,' he said, rubbing the palm of a large calloused hand over the frosted glass of the window.

I let the window down and stuck my head out. There was a cool breeze blowing down the platform, a breeze that whispered of autumn in the hills. As usual there was no activity, except for the fruit-vendor walking up and down the length of the train with his basket of mangoes balanced on his head. At the tea-stall, a kettle was steaming, but there was no one to mind it. I rested my forehead on the window-ledge, and let the breeze play on my temples. I had been feeling sick and giddy but there was a wild sweetness in the wind that I found soothing.

'Yes,' I said to myself, 'I wonder what happens in Shamli, behind the station walls.'

My fellow passenger offered me a bidi. He was a farmer, I think, on his way to Dehra. He had a long, untidy, sad moustache.

We had been more than five minutes at the station. I looked up and down the platform, but nobody was getting on or off the train. Presently, the guard came walking past our compartment.

'What's the delay?' I asked him.

'Some obstruction further down the line,' he said.

'Will we be here long?'

'I don't know what the trouble is. About half an hour, at the least.'

My neighbour shrugged, and, throwing the remains of his bidi out of the window, closed his eyes and immediately fell asleep. I moved restlessly in my seat, and then the man came out of the lavatory, not so urgently now, and with obvious peace of mind. I closed the door for him.

I stood up and stretched; and this stretching of my limbs seemed to set in motion a stretching of the mind, and I found myself thinking: 'I am in no hurry to get to Saharanpur, and I have always wanted to see Shamli, behind the station walls. If I get down now, I can spend the day here, it will be better than sitting in this train for another hour. Then in the evening I can catch the next train home.'

In those days I never had the patience to wait for second thoughts, and so I began pulling my small suitcase out from under the seat.

The farmer woke up and asked, 'What are you doing, brother?'

'I'm getting out,' I said.

He went to sleep again.

It would have taken at least fifteen minutes to reach the door, as people and their belongings cluttered up the passage; so I let my suitcase down from the window and followed it on to the platform.

There was no one to collect my ticket at the barrier, because there was obviously no point in keeping a man there to collect tickets from passengers who never came; and anyway, I had a through-ticket to my destination, which I would need in the evening.

I went out of the station and came to Shamli.

◆

Outside the station there was a neem tree, and under it stood a tonga. The tonga-pony was nibbling at the grass at the foot of the tree. The youth in the front seat was the only human in sight; there were no signs of inhabitants or habitation. I approached the tonga, and the youth stared at me as though he couldn't believe his eyes.

'Where is Shamli?' I asked.

'Why, friend, this is Shamli,' he said.

I looked around again, but couldn't see any signs of life. A dusty road led past the station and disappeared in the forest.

'Does anyone live here?' I asked.

'I live here,' he said, with an engaging smile. He looked an amiable, happy-go-lucky fellow. He wore a cotton tunic and dirty white pyjamas.

'Where?' I asked.

'In my tonga, of course,' he said. 'I have had this pony five years now. I carry supplies to the hotel. But today the manager has not come to collect them. You are going to the hotel? I will take you.'

'Oh, so there's a hotel?'

'Well, friend, it is called that. And there are a few houses too, and some shops, but they are all about a mile from the station. If they were not a mile from here, I would be out of business.'

I felt relieved, but I still had the feeling of having walked into a town consisting of one station, one pony and one man.

'You can take me,' I said. 'I'm staying till this evening.'

He heaved my suitcase into the seat beside him, and I climbed in at the back. He flicked the reins and slapped his pony on the buttocks; and, with a roll and a lurch, the buggy moved off down the dusty forest road.

'What brings you here?' asked the youth.

'Nothing,' I said. 'The train was delayed, I was feeling bored, and so I got off.'

He did not believe that; but he didn't question me further. The sun was reaching up over the forest, but the road lay in the shadow of tall trees, eucalyptus, mango and neem.

'Not many people stay in the hotel,' he said. 'So it is cheap. You will get a room for five rupees.'

'Who is the manager?'

'Mr Satish Dayal. It is his father's property. Satish Dayal could not pass his exams or get a job, so his father sent him here to look after the hotel.'

The jungle thinned out, and we passed a temple, a mosque, a few small shops. There was a strong smell of burnt sugar in the air, and in the distance I saw a factory chimney: that, then, was the reason for Shamli's existence. We passed a bullock-cart laden with sugarcane. The road went through fields of cane and maize, and then, just as we were about to re-enter the jungle, the youth pulled his horse to a side road and the hotel came in sight.

It was a small white bungalow, with a garden in the front, banana trees at the sides, and an orchard of guava trees at the back. We came jingling up to the front verandah. Nobody appeared, nor was there any sign of life on the premises.

'They are all asleep,' said the youth.

I said, 'I'll sit in the verandah and wait.' I got down from the tonga, and the youth dropped my case on the verandah steps. Then he stood in front of me, smiling amiably, waiting to be paid.

'Well, how much?' I asked.

'As a friend, only one rupee.'

'That's too much,' I complained. 'This is not Delhi.'

'This is Shamli,' he said. 'I am the only tonga-driver in Shamli. You may not pay me anything, if that is your wish. But then, I will not take you back to the station this evening, you will have to walk.'

I gave him the rupee. He had both charm and cunning, an effective combination.

'Come in the evening at about six,' I said.

'I will come,' he said, with an infectious smile, 'Don't worry.'

I waited till the tonga had gone round the bend in the road before walking up the verandah steps.

The doors of the house were closed, and there were no bells to ring. I didn't have a watch, but I judged the time to be a little past six o'clock. The hotel didn't look very impressive; the whitewash was coming off the walls, and the cane-chairs on the verandah were old and crooked. A stag's head was mounted over the front door, but one of its glass eyes had fallen out. I had often heard hunters speak of how beautiful an animal looked before it died, but how could anyone with a true love of the beautiful care for the stuffed head of an animal, grotesquely mounted, with no resemblance to its living aspect?

I felt too restless to take any of the chairs. I began pacing up and down the verandah, wondering if I should start banging on the doors. Perhaps the hotel was deserted; perhaps the tonga-driver had played a trick on me. I began to regret my impulsiveness in leaving the train. When I saw the manager I would have to invent a reason for coming to his hotel. I was good at inventing reasons. I would tell him that a friend of mine had stayed here some years ago, and that I was trying to trace him. I decided that my friend would have to be a little eccentric (having chosen Shamli to live in), that he had become a recluse, shutting himself off from the world; his parents—no, his sister—for his parents would be dead—had asked me to find him if I could; and, as he had last been heard of in Shamli, I had taken the opportunity to enquire after him. His name would be Major Roberts, retired.

I heard a tap running at the side of the building, and walking around, found a young man bathing at the tap. He was strong and well-built, and slapped himself on the body with great enthusiasm. He had not seen me approaching, and I waited until he had finished bathing and had began to dry himself.

'Hullo,' I said.

He turned at the sound of my voice, and looked at me for a few moments with a puzzled expression; he had a round, cheerful face and crisp black hair. He smiled slowly, but it was a more genuine smile than the tonga-driver's. So far I had met two people in Shamli, and they were both smilers; that should have cheered me, but it didn't. 'You have come to stay?' he asked, in a slow easygoing voice.

'Just for the day,' I said. 'You work here?'

'Yes, my name is Daya Ram. The manager is asleep just now, but I will find a room for you.'

He pulled on his vest and pyjamas, and accompanied me back to the verandah. Here he picked up my suitcase and, unlocking a side door, led me into the house. We went down a passageway; then Daya Ram stopped at the door on the right, pushed it open, and took me into a small, sunny room that had a window looking out on the orchard. There was a bed, a desk, a couple of cane-chairs, and a frayed and faded red carpet.

'Is it alright?' asked Daya Ram.

'Perfectly alright.'

'They have breakfast at eight o'clock. But if you are hungry, I will make something for you now.'

'No, it's alright. Are you the cook too?'

'I do everything here.'

'Do you like it?'

'No,' he said, and then added, in a sudden burst of confidence, 'There are no women for a man like me.'

'Why don't you leave, then?'

'I will,' he said, with a doubtful look on his face. 'I will leave...'

After he had gone I shut the door and went into the bathroom to bathe. The cold water refreshed me and made me feel one with the world. After I had dried myself, I sat on the bed, in front of the open window. A cool breeze, smelling of rain, came through the window and played over my body. I thought I saw a movement among the trees.

And getting closer to the window, I saw a girl on a swing. She was a small girl, all by herself, and she was swinging to and fro, and singing, and her song carried faintly on the breeze.

I dressed quickly, and left my room. The girl's dress was billowing in the breeze, her pigtails flying about. When she saw me approaching, she stopped swinging, and stared at me. I stopped a little distance away.

'Who are you?' she asked.

'A ghost,' I replied.

'You look like one,' she said.

I decided to take this as a compliment, as I was determined to make friends. I did not smile at her, because some children dislike adults who smile at them all the time.

'What's your name?' I asked.

'Kiran,' she said, 'I'm ten.'

'You are getting old.'

'Well, we all have to grow old one day. Aren't you coming any closer?'

'May I?' I asked.

'You may. You can push the swing.'

One pigtail lay across the girl's chest; the other behind her shoulder. She had a serious face, and obviously felt she had responsibilities; she seemed to be in a hurry to grow up, and I suppose she had no time for anyone who treated her as a child. I pushed the swing, until it went higher and higher, and then I stopped pushing, so that she came lower each time and we could talk.

'Tell me about the people who live here,' I said.

'There is Heera,' she said. 'He's the gardener. He's nearly a hundred. You can see him behind the hedges in the garden. You can't see him unless you look hard. He tells me stories—a new story every day. He's much better than the people in the hotel, and so is Daya Ram.'

'Yes, I met Daya Ram.'

'He's my bodyguard. He brings me nice things from the kitchen when no one is looking.'

'You don't stay here?'

'No, I live in another house; you can't see it from here. My father is the manager of the factory.'

'Aren't there any other children to play with?' I asked.

'I don't know any,' she said.

'And the people staying here?'

'Oh, they.' Apparently Kiran didn't think much of the hotel guests. 'Miss Deeds is funny when she's drunk. And Mr Lin is the strangest.'

'And what about the manager, Mr Dayal?'

'He's mean. And he gets frightened of slightest things. But Mrs Dayal is nice; she lets me take flowers home. But she doesn't talk much.'

I was fascinated by Kiran's ruthless summing up of the guests. I brought the swing to a standstill and asked, 'And what do you think of me?'

'I don't know as yet,' said Kiran quite seriously. 'I'll think about you.'

◆

As I came back to the hotel, I heard the sound of a piano in one of the front rooms. I didn't know enough about music to be able to recognize the piece, but it had sweetness and melody, though it was played with some hesitancy. As I came nearer, the sweetness deserted the music, probably because the piano was out of tune.

The person at the piano had distinctive Mongolian features, and so I presumed he was Mr Lin. He hadn't seen me enter the room, and I stood beside the curtains of the door, watching him play. He had full round lips and high, slanting cheekbones. His eyes were large and round and full of melancholy. His long, slender fingers hardly touched the keys.

I came nearer; and then he looked up at me, without any show of surprise or displeasure, and kept on playing.

'What are you playing?' I asked.

'Chopin,' he said.

'Oh, yes. It's nice, but the piano is fighting it.'

'I know. This piano belonged to one of Kipling's aunts. It hasn't been tuned since the last century.'

'Do you live here?'

'No, I come from Calcutta,' he answered readily. 'I have some business here with the sugarcane people actually, though I am not a businessman.' He was playing softly all the time, so that our conversation was not lost in the music. 'I don't know anything about business. But I have to do something.'

'Where did you learn to play the piano?'

'In Singapore. A French lady taught me. She had great hopes of my becoming a concert pianist when I grew up. I would have toured Europe and America.'

'Why didn't you?'

'We left during the War, and I had to give up my lessons.'

'And why did you go to Calcutta?'

'My father is a Calcutta businessman. What do you do, and why do you come here?' he asked. 'If I am not being too inquisitive.'

Before I could answer, a bell rang, loud and continuously, drowning the music and conversation.

'Breakfast,' said Mr Lin.

A thin dark man, wearing glasses, stepped nervously into the room and peered at me in an anxious manner.

'You arrived last night?'

'That's right,' I said, 'I just want to stay the day. I think you're the manager?'

'Yes. Would you like to sign the register?'

I went with him past the bar and into the office. I wrote my name and Mussoorie address in the register, and the duration of my stay. I paused at the column marked 'Profession', thought it would be best to fill it with something and wrote 'Author'.

'You are here on business?' asked Mr Dayal.

'No, not exactly. You see, I'm looking for a friend of mine who was heard of in Shamli, about three years ago. I thought I'd make a few enquiries in case he's still here.'

'What was his name? Perhaps he stayed here.'

'Major Roberts,' I said. 'An Anglo-Indian.'

'Well, you can look through the old registers after breakfast.'

He accompanied me into the dining-room. The establishment was really more of a boarding-house than a hotel, because Mr Dayal ate with his guests. There was a round mahogany dining-table in the centre of the room, and Mr Lin was the only one seated at it. Daya Ram hovered about with plates and trays. I took my seat next to Lin, and, as I did so, a door opened from the passage, and a woman of about thirty-five came in.

She had on a skirt and blouse, which accentuated a firm, well-rounded figure, and she walked on high-heels, with a rhythmical swaying of the hips. She had an uninteresting face, camouflaged with lipstick, rouge and powder—the powder so thick that is had become embedded in the natural lines of her face—but her figure compelled admiration.

'Miss Deeds,' whispered Lin.

There was a false note to her greeting.

'Hallo, everyone,' she said heartily, straining for effect. 'Why are you all so quiet? Has Mr Lin been playing the Funeral March again? She sat down and continued talking. 'Really, we must have a dance or something to liven things up. You must know some good numbers Lin, after your experience in Singapore night-clubs. What's for breakfast? Boiled eggs. Daya Ram, can't you make an omelette for a change? I know you're not a professional cook, but you don't have to give us the same thing every day, and there's absolutely no reason why you should burn the toast. You'll have to do something about a cook, Mr Dayal.' Then she noticed me sitting opposite her. 'Oh, hallo,' she said, genuinely surprised. She gave me a long appraising look.

'This gentleman,' said Mr Dayal introducing me, 'is an author.'

'That's nice,' said Miss Deeds. 'Are you married?'

'No,' I said. 'Are you?'

'Funny, isn't it,' she said, without taking offence, 'No one in this house seems to be married.'

'I'm married,' said Mr Dayal.

'Oh, yes, of course,' said Miss Deeds. 'And what brings you to Shamli?' she asked, turning to me.

'I'm looking for a friend called Major Roberts.'

Lin gave an exclamation of surprise. I thought he had seen through my deception.

But another game had begun.

'I knew him,' said Lin. 'A great friend of mine.'

◆

'Yes,' continued Lin. 'I knew him. A good chap, Major Roberts.'

Well, there I was, inventing people to suit my convenience, and people like Mr Lin started inventing relationships with them. I was too intrigued to try and discourage him. I wanted to see how far he would go.

'When did you meet him?' asked Lin, taking the initiative.

'Oh, only about three years back. Just before he disappeared. He was last heard of in Shamli.'

'Yes, I heard he was here,' said Lin. 'But he went away, when he thought his relatives had traced him. He went into the mountains near Tibet.'

'Did he?' I said, unwilling to be instructed further. 'What part of the country? I come from the hills myself. I know the Mana and Niti passes quite well. If you have any idea of exactly where he went. I think I could find him.' I had the advantage in this exchange, because I was the one who had originally invented Roberts. Yet I couldn't bring myself to end his deception, probably because I felt sorry for him. A happy man wouldn't take the trouble of inventing friendships with people who didn't exist; he'd be too busy with friends who did.

'You've had a lonely life, Mr Lin?' I asked.

'Lonely?' said Mr Lin, with forced incredulousness. 'I'd never been lonely till I came here a month ago. When I was in Singapore—'

'You never get any letters though, do you?' asked Miss Deeds suddenly.

Lin was silent for a moment. Then he said, 'Do you?'

Miss Deeds lifted her head a little, as a horse does when it is annoyed, and I thought her pride had been hurt; but then she laughed unobstrusively and tossed her head.

'I never write letters,' she said. 'My friends gave me up as hopeless years ago. They know it's no use writing to me, because they rarely get a reply. They call me the Jungle Princess.'

Mr Dayal tittered, and I found it hard to suppress a smile. To cover up my smile I asked, 'You teach here?'

'Yes, I teach at the girl's school,' she said with a frown. 'But don't talk to me about teaching. I have enough of it all day.'

'You don't like teaching?'

She gave an aggressive look. 'Should I?' she asked.

'Shouldn't you?' I said.

She paused, and then said, 'Who are you, anyway, the Inspector of Schools?'

'No,' said Mr Dayal who wasn't following very well. 'He's a journalist.'

'I've heard they are nosey,' said Miss Deeds.

Once again Lin interrupted to steer the conversation away from a delicate issue.

'Where's Mrs Dayal this morning?' asked Lin.

'She spent the night with our neighbours,' said Mr Dayal. 'She should be here after lunch.'

It was the first time Mrs Dayal had been mentioned. Nobody spoke either well or ill of her; I suspected that she kept her distance from the others, avoiding familiarity. I began to wonder about Mrs Dayal.

◆

Daya Ram came in from the verandah, looking worried.

'Heera's dog has disappeared,' he said. 'He thinks a leopard took it.'

Heera, the gardener was standing respectfully outside on the verandah steps. We all hurried out to him, firing questions which he didn't try to answer.

'Yes. It's a leopard' said Kiran, appearing from behind Heera. 'It's going to come into the hotel,' she added cheerfully.

'Be quiet,' said Satish Dayal crossly.

'There are pug marks under the trees,' said Daya Ram.

Mr Dayal, who seemed to know little about leopards or pug marks, said, 'I will take a look', and led the way to the orchard, the rest of us trailing behind in an ill-assorted procession.

There were marks on the soft earth in the orchard (they could have been a leopard's), which went in the direction of the riverbed. Mr Dayal paled a little and went hurrying back to the hotel. Heera returned to the front garden, the least excited, the most sorrowful. Everyone else was thinking of a leopard, but he was thinking of the dog.

I followed him, and watched him weeding the sunflower beds. His face wrinkled like a walnut, but his eyes were clear and bright. His hands were thin and bony, but there was a deftness and power in the wrist and fingers, and the weeds flew fast from his spade. He had cracked, parchment-like skin. I could not help thinking of the gloss and glow of Daya Ram's limbs, as I had seen them when he was bathing, and wondered if Heera's had once been like that and if Daya Ram's would ever be like this, and both possibilities—or were they probabilities?—saddened me. Our skin, I thought, is like the leaf of a tree, young and green and shiny; then it gets darker and heavier, sometimes spotted with disease, sometimes eaten away; then fading, yellow and red, then falling, crumbling into dust or feeding the flames of fire. I looked at my own skin, still smooth, not coarsened by labour; I thought of Kiran's fresh rose-tinted complexion; Miss Deed's skin, hard and dry; Lin's pale taut skin, stretched tightly across his prominent cheeks and forehead; and Mr Dayal' s grey skin, growing thick hair. And I wondered about Mrs Dayal and the kind of skin she would have.

'Did you have the dog for long?' I asked Heera.

He looked up with surprise, for he had been unaware of my presence.

'Six years, sahib,' he said. 'He was not a clever dog, but he was very friendly. He followed me home one day, when I was coming back from the bazaar. I kept telling him to go away, but he wouldn't. It was a long walk and so I began talking to him. I liked talking to him, and I have always talked with him, and we have understood each other. That first night, when I came home, I shut the gate between us. But he stood on the other side, looking at me with trusting eyes. Why did he have to look at me like that?'

'So, you kept him?'

'Yes, I could never forget the way he looked at me. I shall feel lonely now, because he was my only companion. My wife and son died long ago. It seems I am to stay here forever, until everyone has gone, until there are only ghosts in Shamli. Already the ghosts are here...'

I heard a light footfall behind me and turned to find Kiran. The bare-footed girl stood beside the gardener, and with her toes, began to pull at the weeds.

'You are a lazy one,' said the old man. 'If you want to help me, sit down and use your hands.'

I looked at the girl's fair round face, and in her bright eyes I saw something old and wise; and I looked into the old man's wise eyes, and saw something forever bright and young. The skin cannot change the eyes; the eyes are the true reflection of a man's age and sensibilities; even a blind man has hidden eyes.

'I hope we shall find the dog,' said Kiran. 'But I would like a leopard. Nothing ever happens here.'

'Not now,' sighed Heera. 'Not now... Why, once there was a band and people danced till morning, but now...'

'I have always been here,' said Heera. 'I was here before Shamli.'

'Before the station?'

'Before there was a station, or a factory, or a bazaar. It was a village then, and the only way to get here was by bullock-cart. Then a bus service was started, then the railway lines were laid and a station built, then they started the sugar factory, and for a few years Shamli was a town. But the jungle was bigger than the town. The rains were heavy and malaria was everywhere. People didn't stay long in Shamli. Gradually, they went back into the hills. Sometimes I too want to go back to the hills, but what is the use when you are old and have no one left in the world except a few flowers in a troublesome garden. I had to choose between the flowers and the hills, and I chose the flowers. I am tired now, and old, but I am not tired of flowers.'

I could see that his real world was the garden; there was more variety in his flower-beds than there was in the town of Shamli. Every month, every day, there were new flowers in the garden, but there were always the same people in Shamli.

I left Kiran with the old man, and returned to my room. It must have been about eleven o'clock.

◆

I was facing the window when I heard my door being opened. Turning, I perceived the barrel of a gun moving slowly round the edge of the door. Behind the gun was Satish Dayal, looking hot and sweaty. I didn't know what his intentions were; so, deciding it would be better to act first and reason later, I grabbed a pillow from the bed and flung it in his face. I then threw myself at his legs and brought him crashing down to the ground.

When we got up, I was holding the gun. It was an old Enfield rifle, probably dating back to the Afghan wars; the kind that goes off at the least encouragment.

'But—but—why?' stammered the dishevelled and alarmed Mr Dayal.

'I don't know,' I said menacingly. 'Why did you come in here pointing this at me?'

'I wasn't pointing it at you. It's for the leopard.'

'Oh, so you came into my room looking for a leopard? You have, I presume, been stalking one about the hotel?' (By now I was convinced that Mr Dayal had taken leave of his senses and was hunting imaginary leopards.)

'No, no,' cried the distraught man, becoming more confused, 'I was looking for you. I wanted to ask you if you could use a gun. I was thinking we should go looking for the leopard that took Heera's dog. Neither Mr Lin nor I can shoot.'

'Your gun is not up-to-date.' I said. 'It's not at all suitable for hunting leopards. A stout stick would be more effective. Why don't we arm ourselves with lathis and make a general assault?'

I said this banteringly, but Mr Dayal took the idea quite seriously. 'Yes, yes,' he said with alacrity, 'Daya Ram has got one or two lathis in the godown. The three of us could make an expedition. I have asked Mr Lin but he says he doesn't want to have anything to do with leopards.'

'What about our Jungle Princess?' I said. 'Miss Deeds should be pretty good with a lathi.'

'Yes, yes,' said Mr Dayal humourlessly, 'but we'd better not ask her.'

Collecting Daya Ram and two lathis, we set off for the orchard and began following the pug marks through the trees. It took us ten minutes to reach the riverbed, a dry hot rocky place; then we went into the jungle, Mr Dayal keeping well to the rear. The atmosphere was heavy and humid, and there was not a breath of air amongst the trees. When a parrot squawked suddenly, shattering the silence, Mr Dayal let out a startled exclamation and started for home.

'What was that?' he asked nervously.

'A bird,' I explained.

'I think we should go back now,' he said, 'I don't think the leopard's here.'

'You never know with leopards,' I said, 'They could be anywhere.'

Mr Dayal stepped away from the bushes. 'I'll have to go,' he said. 'I have a lot of work. You keep a lathi with you, and I'll send Daya Ram back later.'

'That's very thoughtful of you,' I said.

Daya Ram scratched his head and reluctantly followed his employer back through the trees. I moved on slowly down the little-used path, wondering if I should also return. I saw two monkeys playing on the branch of a tree, and decided that there could be no danger in the immediate vicinity.

Presently I came to a clearing where there was a pool of fresh clear water. It was fed by a small stream that came suddenly, like a snake, out of the long grass. The water looked cool and inviting; laying down the lathi and taking off my clothes, I ran down the bank until I was waist-deep in the middle of the pool. I splashed about for some time, before emerging; then I lay on the soft grass and allowed the sun to dry my body. I closed my eyes and gave myself up to beautiful thoughts. I had forgotten all about leopards.

I must have slept for about half an hour because when I awoke, I found that Daya Ram had come back and was vigorously threshing about in the narrow confines of the pool. I sat up and asked him the time.

'Twelve o'clock,' he shouted, coming out of water, his dripping body all gold and silver in sunlight. 'They will be waiting for dinner.'

'Let them wait,' I said.

It was a relief to talk to Daya Ram, after the uneasy conversations in the lounge and dining-room.

'Dayal sahib will be angry with me.'

'I'll tell him we found the trail of the leopard, and that we went so far into the jungle that we lost our way. As Miss Deeds is so critical of the food, let her cook the meal.'

'Oh, she only talks like that,' said Daya Ram. 'Inside she is very soft. She is too soft in some ways.'

'She should be married.'

'Well, she would like to be. Only there is no one to marry her. When she came here she was engaged to be married to an English army captain; I think she loved him, but she is the sort of person who cannot help loving many men all at once, and the captain could not understand that—it is just the way she is made,

I suppose. She is always ready to fall in love.'

'You seem to know,' I said.

'Oh, yes.'

We dressed and walked back to the hotel. In a few hours, I thought, the tonga will come for me and I will be back at the station; the mysterious charm of Shamli will be no more, but whenever I pass this way I will wonder about these people, about Miss Deeds and Lin and Mrs Dayal.

Mrs Dayal... She was the one person I was yet to meet; it was with some excitement and curiosity that I looked forward to meeting her; she was about the only mystery left to Shamli, now, and perhaps she would be no mystery when I met her. And yet... I felt that perhaps she would justify the impulse that made me get down from the train.

I could have asked Daya Ram about Mrs Dayal, and so satisfied my curiosity; but I wanted to discover her for myself. Half the day was left to me, and I didn't want my game to finish too early.

I walked towards the verandah, and the sound of the piano came through the open door.

'I wish Mr Lin would play something cheerful,' said Miss Deeds. 'He's obsessed with the Funeral March. Do you dance?'

'Oh no,' I said.

She looked disappointed. But when Lin left the piano, she went into the lounge and sat down on the stool. I stood at the door watching her, wondering what she would do.

Lin left the room, somewhat resentfully.

She began to play an old song, which I remembered having heard in a film or on a gramophone record. She sang while she played, in a slightly harsh but pleasant voice:

Rolling round the world
Looking for the sunshine
I know I'm going to find some day...

Then she played 'Am I blue?' and 'Darling, Je Vous Aime Beaucoup'. She sat there singing in a deep husky voice, her eyes a little misty, her hard face suddenly kind and sloppy. When the gong rang, she broke off playing, and shook off her sentimental mood, and laughed derisively at herself.

I don't remember that lunch. I hadn't slept much since the previous night and I was beginning to feel the strain of my journey. The swim had refreshed me, but it had also made me drowsy. I ate quite well, though, of rice and kofta curry, and then, feeling sleepy, made for the garden to find a shady tree.

There were some books on the shelf in the lounge, and I ran my eye over them in search of one that might condition sleep. But they were too dull to do even that. So I went into the garden, and there was Kiran on the swing, and I went to her tree and sat down on the grass.

'Did you find the leopard?' she asked.

'No,' I said, with a yawn.

'Tell me a story.'

'You tell me one,' I said.

'Alright. Once there was a lazy man with long legs, who was always yawning and wanting to fall asleep...'

I watched the swaying motions of the swing and the movements of the girl's bare legs, and a tiny insect kept buzzing about in front of my nose... 'and fall asleep, and the reason for this was that he liked to dream.' I blew the insect away, and the swing became hazy and distant, and Kiran was a blurred figure in the trees...

'...liked to dream, and what do you think he dreamt about...?' Dreamt about, dreamt about...

◆

When I awoke there was that cool rain-scented breeze blowing across the garden. I remember lying on the grass with my eyes closed, listening to the swishing of the swing. Either I had not slept long, or Kiran had been a long time on the swing; it was moving slowly now, in a more leisurely fashion, without much sound. I opened my eyes and saw that my arm was stained with the juice of the grass beneath me. Looking up, I expected to see Kiran's legs waving above me. But instead I saw dark slim feet, and above them the folds of a sari. I straightened up against the trunk of the tree to look closer at Kiran, but Kiran wasn't there, it was someone else on the swing, a young woman in a pink sari and with a red rose in her hair.

She had stopped the swing with her foot on the ground, and she was smiling at me.

It wasn't a smile you could see, it was a tender fleeting movement that came suddenly and was gone at the same time, and its going was sad. I thought of the others' smiles, just as I had thought of their skins: the tonga-driver's friendly, deceptive grin; Daya Ram's wide sincere smile; Miss Deed's cynical, derisive smile. And looking at Sushila, I knew a smile could never change. She had always smiled that way.

'You haven't changed,' she said.

I was standing up now, though still leaning against the tree for support. Though I had never thought much about the *sound* of her voice, it seemed as familiar as the sounds of yesterday.

'You haven't changed either,' I said. 'But where did you come from?' I wasn't sure yet if I was awake or dreaming.

She laughed, as she had always laughed at me.

'I came from behind the tree. The little girl has gone.'

'Yes, I'm dreaming,' I said helplessly.

'But what brings you here?'

'I don't know. At least I didn't know when I came. But it must have been you. The train stopped at Shamli, and I don't know why, but I decided I would spend the day here, behind the station walls.

You must be married now, Sushila.'

'Yes, I am married to Mr Dayal, the manager of the hotel. And what has been happening with you?'

'I am still a writer, still poor, and still living in Mussoorie.'

'When were you last in Delhi?' she asked. 'I don't mean Delhi, I mean at home.'

'I have not been to your home since you were there.'

'Oh, my friend,' she said, getting up suddenly and coming to me, 'I want to talk to you. I want to talk about our home and Sunil and our friends and all those things that are so far away now. I have been here two years, and I am already feeling old. I keep remembering our home, how young I was, how happy, and I am all alone with memories. But now *you* are here! It was a bit of magic, I came through the trees after Kiran had gone, and there you were, fast asleep under the tree. I didn't wake you then, because I wanted to see you wake up.'

'As I used to watch you wake up...'

She was near me and I could look at her more closely. Her cheeks did not have the same freshness; they were a little pale, and she was thinned now, but her eyes were the same, smiling the same way. Her voice was the same. Her fingers, when she took my hand, were the same warm delicate fingers.

'Talk to me,' she said. 'Tell me about yourself.'

'You tell me,' I said.

'I am here,' she said. 'That is all there is about myself.'

'Then let us sit down and I'll talk.'

'Not here.' She took my hand and led me through the trees. 'Come with me.'

I heard the jingle of a tonga-bell and a faint shout; I stopped and laughed.

'My tonga,' I said. 'It has come to take me back to the station.'

'But you are not going,' said Sushila, immediately downcast.

'I will tell him to come in the morning,' I said. 'I will spend the night in your Shamli.'

I walked to the front of the hotel where the tonga was waiting. I was glad no one else was in sight. The youth was smiling at me in his most appealing manner.

'I'm not going today,' I said. 'Will you come tomorrow morning?'

'I can come whenever you like, friend. But you will have to pay for every trip, because it is a long way from the station even if my tonga is empty.'

'Alright, how much?'

'Usual fare, friend, one rupee.'

I didn't try to argue but resignedly gave him the rupee. He cracked his whip and pulled on the reins, and the carriage moved off.

'If you don't leave tomorrow,' the youth called out after me, 'you'll never leave Shamli!'

I walked back to the trees, but I couldn't find Sushila.

'Sushila, where are you?' I called, but I might have been speaking to the trees, for I had no reply. There was a small path going through the orchard, and on the path I saw a rose petal. I walked a little further and saw another petal. They were from Sushila's red rose. I walked on down the path until I had skirted the orchard, and then the path went along the fringe of the jungle, past a clump of bamboos, and here the grass was a lush green as though it had been constantly watered. I was still finding rose petals. I heard the chatter of seven sisters, and the call of hoopoe. The path bent to meet a stream; there was a willow coming down to the water's edge, and Sushila was waiting there.

'Why didn't you wait?' I said.

'I wanted to see if you were as good at following me as you used to be.'

'Well, I am,' I said, sitting down beside her on the grassy bank of the stream. 'Even if I'm out of practice.'

'Yes, I remember the time you climbed onto an apple tree to pick some fruit for me. You got up alright but then you couldn't come down again. I had to climb up myself and help you.'

'I don't remember that,' I said.

'Of course you do.'

'It must have been your other friend, Pramod.'

'I never climbed trees with Pramod.'

'Well, I don't remember.'

I looked at the little stream that ran past us. The water was no more than ankle-deep, cold and clear and sparkling, like the mountain-stream near my home. I took off my shoes, rolled up my trousers, and put my feet in water. Sushila's feet joined mine.

At first I had wanted to ask her about her marriage, whether she was happy or not, what she thought of her husband; but now I couldn't ask her these things, they seemed far away and of little importance. I could think of nothing she had in common with Mr Dayal; I felt that her charm and attractiveness and warmth could not have been appreciated, or even noticed, by that curiously distracted man. He was much older than her, of course; probably older than me; he was obviously not her choice but her parents'; and so far they were childless. Had there been children, I don't think Sushila would have minded Mr Dayal as her husband. Children would have made up for the absence of passion—or was there passion in Satish Dayal? I remembered having heard that Sushila had been married to a man she didn't like; I remembered having shrugged off the news, because it meant she would never come my way again, and I have never yearned after something that has been irredeemably lost. But she had come my way again. And was she still lost? That was what I wanted to know...

'What do you do with yourself all day?' I asked.

'Oh, I visit the school and help with the classes. It is the only interest I have in this place. The hotel is terrible. I try to keep away from it as much as I can.'

'And what about the guests?'

'Oh, don't let us talk about them. Let us talk about ourselves. Do you have to go tomorrow?'

'Yes, I suppose so. Will you always be in this place?'

'I suppose so.'

That made me silent. I took her hand, and my feet churned up the mud at the bottom of the stream. As the mud subsided, I saw Sushila's face reflected in the water; and looking up at her again, into her dark eyes, the old yearning returned and I wanted to care for her and protect her, I wanted to take her away from that place, from sorrowful Shamli; I wanted her to live again. Of course, I had forgotten all about my poor finances, Sushila's family, and the shoes I wore, which were my last pair. The uplift I was experiencing in this meeting with Sushila, who had always, throughout her childhood and youth, bewitched me as no other had ever bewitched me, made me reckless and impulsive.

I lifted her hand to my lips and kissed her in the soft of the palm.

'Can I kiss you?' I said.

'You have just done so.'

'Can I kiss you?' I repeated.

'It is not necessary.'

I leaned over and kissed her slender neck. I knew she would like this, because that was where I had kissed her often before. I kissed her in the soft of the throat, where it tickled.

'It is not necessary,' she said, but she ran her fingers through my hair and let them rest there. I kissed her behind the ear then, and kept my mouth to her ear and whispered, 'Can I kiss you?'

She turned her face to me so that we were deep in each other's eyes, and I kissed her again, and we put our arms around each other and lay together on the grass, with the water running over our feet; and we said nothing at all, simply lay there for what seemed like several years, or until the first drop of rain.

It was a big wet drop, and it splashed on Sushila's cheek, just next to mine, and ran down to her lips, so that I had to kiss her again. The next big drop splattered on the tip of my nose, and Sushila laughed and sat up. Little ringlets were forming on the stream where the raindrops hit the water, and above us there was a pattering on the banana leaves.

'We must go,' said Sushila.

We started homewards, but had not gone far before it was raining steadily, and Sushila's hair came loose and streamed down her body. The rain fell harder, and we had to hop over pools and avoid the soft mud. Sushila's sari was plastered to her body, accentuating her ripe, thrusting breasts, and I was excited to passion, and pulled her beneath a big tree and crushed her in my arms and kissed her rain-kissed mouth. And then I thought she was crying, but I wasn't sure, because it might have been the raindrops on her cheeks.

'Come away with me,' I said. 'Leave this place. Come away with me tomorrow morning. We will go somewhere where nobody will know us or come between us.'

She smiled at me and said, 'You are still a dreamer, aren't you?'

'Why can't you come?'

'I am married; it is as simple as that.'

'If it is that simple, you can come.'

'I have to think of my parents, too. It would break my father's heart if I were to do what you are proposing. And you are proposing it without a thought for the consequences.'

'You are too practical.' I said.

'If women were not practical, most marriages would be failures.'

'So, your marriage is a success?'

'Of course it is, as a marriage. I am not happy and I do not love him, but neither am I so unhappy that I should hate him. Sometimes, for our own sakes, we have to think of the happiness of others. What happiness would we have living in hiding from everyone we once knew and cared for? Don't be a fool. I am always here and you can come to see me, and nobody will be made unhappy by it. But take me away and we will only have regrets.'

'You don't love me,' I said foolishly.

'That sad word love,' she said, and became pensive and silent.

I could say no more. I was angry again, and rebellious, and there was no one and nothing to rebel against. I could not understand someone who was afraid to break away from an unhappy existence lest that existence should become unhappier; I had always considered it an admirable thing to break away from security and respectability. Of course it is easier for a man to do this, a man can look after himself, he can do without neighbours and the approval of the local society. A woman, I reasoned, would do anything for love provided it was not at the price of security; for a woman loves security as much as a man loves independence.

'I must go back now,' said Sushila. 'You follow a little later.'

'All you wanted to do was talk,' I complained.

She laughed at that, and pulled me playfully by the hair; then she ran out from under the tree, springing across the grass, and the wet mud flew up and flecked her legs. I watched her through the thin curtain of rain, until she reached the verandah. She turned to wave to me, and then skipped into the hotel. She was still young; but I was no younger.

◆

The rain had lessened, but I didn't know what to do with myself. The hotel was uninviting, and it was too late to leave Shamli. If the grass hadn't been wet I would have preferred to sleep under a tree rather than return to the hotel to sit at that alarming dining-table.

I came out from under the trees and crossed the garden. But instead of making for the verandah I went round to the back of the hotel. Smoke issuing from the barred window of a back room told me I had probably found the kitchen. Daya Ram was inside, squatting in front of a stove, stirring a pot of stew. The stew smelt appetizing. Daya Ram looked up and smiled at me.

'I thought you must have gone,' he said.

'I'll go in the morning,' I said pulling myself upon an empty table. Then I had one of my sudden ideas and said, 'Why don't you come with me? I can find you a good job in Mussoorie. How much do you get paid here?'

'Fifty rupees a month. But I haven't been paid for three months.'

'Could you get your pay before tomorrow morning?'

'No, I won't get anything until one of the guests pays a bill. Miss Deeds owes about fifty rupees on whisky alone. She will pay up, she says, when the school pays her salary. And the school can't pay her until they collect the children's fees. That is how bankrupt everyone is in Shamli.'

'I see,' I said, though I didn't see. 'But Mr Dayal can't hold back your pay just because his guests haven't paid their bills.'

'He can, if he hasn't got any money.'

'I see,' I said, 'Anyway, I will give you my address. You can come when you are free.'

'I will take it from the register,' he said.

I edged over to the stove and, leaning over, sniffed at the stew. 'I'll eat mine now,' I said; and without giving Daya Ram a chance to object, I lifted a plate off the shelf, took hold of the stirring-spoon and helped myself from the pot.

'There's rice too.' said Daya Ram.

I filled another plate with rice and then got busy with my

fingers. After ten minutes, I had finished. I sat back comfortably in the hotel, in ruminative mood. With my stomach full I could take a more tolerant view of life and people. I could understand Sushila's apprehensions, Lin's delicate lying, and Miss Deed's aggressiveness. Daya Ram went out to sound the dinner-gong, and I trailed back to my room.

From the window of my room I saw Kiran running across the lawn, and I called to her, but she didn't hear me. She ran down the path and out of the gate, her pigtails beating against the wind.

The clouds were breaking and coming together again, twisting and spiralling their way across a violet sky. The sun was going down behind the Siwaliks. The sky there was blood-shot. The tall slim trunks of the eucalyptus tree were tinged with an orange glow; the rain had stopped, and the wind was a soft, sullen puff, drifting sadly through the trees. There was a steady drip of water from the eaves of the roof on to the window-sill. Then the sun went down behind the old, old hills, and I remembered my own hills, far beyond these.

The room was dark but I did not turn on the light. I stood near the window, listening to the garden. There was a frog warbling somewhere, and there was a sudden flap of wings overhead. Tomorrow morning I would go, and perhaps I would come back to Shamli one day, and perhaps not; I could always come here looking for Major Roberts, and, who knows, one day I might find him. What should he be like, this lost man? A romantic, a man with a dream, a man with brown skin and blue eyes, living in a hut on a snowy mountain-top, chopping wood and catching fish and swimming in cold mountain streams; a rough, free man with a kind heart and a shaggy beard, a man who owed allegiance to no one, who gave a damn for money and politics and cities, and civilizations, who was his own master, who lived at one with nature knowing no fear. But that was not Major Roberts—that was the man I wanted to be. He was not a Frenchman or an Englishman, he was me, a dream of myself. If only I could find Major Roberts.

When Daya Ram knocked on the door and told me the others had finished dinner, I left my room and made for the lounge. It was quite lively in the lounge. Satish Dayal was at the bar, Lin at the piano, and Miss Deeds in the centre of the room, executing a tango on her own. It was obvious she had been drinking heavily.

'All on credit,' complained Mr Dayal to me. 'I don't know when I'll be paid, but I don't dare to refuse her anything for fear she starts breaking up the hotel.'

'She could do that, too,' I said. 'It comes down without much encouragement.'

Lin began to play a waltz (I think it was waltz), and then I found Miss Deeds in front of me, saying 'Wouldn't you like to dance, old boy?'

'Thank you,' I said, somewhat alarmed. 'I hardly know how to.'

'Oh, come on, be a sport,' she said, pulling me away from the bar. I was glad Sushila wasn't present; she wouldn't have minded, but she'd have laughed as she always laughed when I made a fool of myself.

We went round the floor in what I suppose was waltz-time, though all I did was mark time to Miss Deeds' motions; we were not very steady—this was because I was trying to keep her at arm's length, whilst she was determined to have me crushed to her bosom. At length, Lin finished the waltz. Giving him a grateful look, I pulled myself free. Miss Deeds went over to the piano, leant right across it, and said, 'Play some lively, dear Mr Lin, play some hot stuff.'

To my surprise, Mr Lin, without so much as an expression of distaste or amusement, began to execute what I suppose was the frug or the jitterbug. I was glad she hadn't asked me to dance that one with her.

It all appeared very incongruous to me: Miss Deeds letting herself go in crazy abandonment, Lin playing the piano with great seriousness, and Mr Dayal watching from the bar with an anxious frown. I wondered what Sushila would have thought of them now.

Eventually, Miss Deeds collapsed on the couch breathing heavily. 'Give me a drink,' she cried.

With the noblest of intentions I took her a glass of water. Miss Deeds took a sip and made a face. 'What's this stuff?' she asked. 'It is different.'

'Water,' I said.

'No,' she said, 'now don't joke, tell me what it is.'

'It's water, I assure you,' I said.

When she saw that I was serious, her face coloured up, and I thought she would throw the water at me; but she was too tired to do this, and contented herself by throwing the glass over her shoulder. Mr Dayal made a dive for the flying glass, but he wasn't in time to rescue it, and it hit the wall and fell to pieces on the floor.

Mr Dayal wrung his hands. 'You'd better take her to her room,' he said, as though I were personally responsible for her behaviour just because I'd danced with her.

'I can't carry her alone,' I said, making an unsuccessful attempt at helping Miss Deeds up from the couch.

Mr Dayal called for Daya Ram, and the big amiable youth came lumbering into the lounge. We took an arm each and helped Miss Deeds, feet dragging, across the room. We got her to her room and on to her bed. When we were about to withdraw she said, 'Don't go, my dear, stay with me a little while.'

Daya Ram had discreetly slipped outside. With my hand on the doorknob I said, 'Which of us?'

'Oh, are there two of you?' said Miss Deeds, without a trace of disappointment.

'Yes, Daya Ram helped me carry you here.'

'Oh, and who are you?'

'I'm the writer. You danced with me, remember?'

'Of course. You dance divinely, Mr Writer. Do stay with me. Daya Ram can stay too if he likes.'

I hesitated, my hand on the doorknob. She hadn't opened her eyes all the time I'd been in the room, her arms hung loose, and one bare leg hung over the side of the bed. She was fascinating somehow, and desirable, but I was afraid of her. I went out of the room and quietly closed the door.

◆

As I lay awake in bed I heard the jackal's 'pheau', the cry of fear, which it communicates to all the jungle when there is danger about, a leopard or a tiger. It was a weird howl, and between each note there was a kind of low gurgling. I switched off the light and peered through the closed window. I saw the jackal at the edge of the lawn. It sat almost vertically on its haunches, holding its head straight up to the sky, making the neighbourhood vibrate with the eerie violence of its cries. Then suddenly it started up and ran off into the trees.

Before getting back into bed I made sure the window was fast. The bull-frog was singing again, 'ing-ong; ing-ong', in some foreign language. I wondered if Sushila was awake too, thinking about me. It must have been almost eleven o'clock. I thought of Miss Deeds, with her leg hanging over the edge of the bed. I tossed restlessly, and then sat up. I hadn't slept for two nights but I was not sleepy. I got out of bed without turning on the light and, slowly opening my door, crept down the passageway. I stopped at the door of Miss Deed's room. I stood there listening, but I heard only the ticking of the big clock that might have been in the room or somewhere in the passage. I put my hand on the doorknob, but the door was bolted. That settled the matter.

I would definitely leave Shamli the next morning. Another day in the company of these people and I would be behaving like them. Perhaps I was already doing so! I remembered the tonga-driver's words, 'Don't stay too long in Shamli or you will never leave!'

When the rain came, it was not with a preliminary patter or shower, but all at once, sweeping across the forest like a massive wall, and I could hear it in the trees long before it reached the house. Then it came crashing down on the corrugated roofing, and the hailstones hit the window panes with a hard metallic sound, so that I thought the glass would break. The sound of thunder was like the booming of big guns, and the lightning kept playing over the garden. At every flash of lightning I sighted the swing under the tree, rocking and leaping in the air as though some invisible, agitated being was sitting on it. I wondered about Kiran. Was she sleeping through all this, blissfully unconcerned, or was she lying awake in bed, starting at every clash of thunder, as I was; or was she up and about, exulting in the storm? I half expected to see her come running through the trees, through the rain, to stand on the swing with her hair blowing wild in the wind, laughing at the thunder and the angry skies. Perhaps I did see her, perhaps she was there. I wouldn't have been surprised if she were some forest nymph, living in the hole of a tree, coming out sometimes to play in the garden.

A crash, nearer and louder than any thunder so far, made me sit up in the bed with a start. Perhaps lightning had struck the house. I turned on the switch, but the light didn't come on. A tree must have fallen across the line.

I heard voices in the passage, the voices of several people. I stepped outside to find out what had happened, and started at the appearance of a ghostly apparition right in front of me; it was Mr Dayal standing on the threshold in an oversized pyjama suit, a candle in his hand.

'I came to wake you,' he said. 'This storm.'

He had the irritating habit of stating the obvious.

'Yes, the storm,' I said. 'Why is everybody up?'

'The back wall has collapsed and part of the roof has fallen in. We'd better spend the night in the lounge, it is the safest room. This is a very old building,' he added apologetically.

'Alright,' I said. 'I am coming.'

The lounge was lit by two candles; one stood over the piano, the other on a small table near the couch. Miss Deeds was on the couch, Lin was at the piano-stool, looking as though he would start playing Stravinsky any moment, and Mr Dayal was fussing about the room. Sushila was standing at a window, looking out at the stormy night. I went to the window and touched her, She didn't look round or say anything. The lightning flashed and her dark eyes were pools of smouldering fire.

'What time will you be leaving?' she said.

'The tonga will come for me at seven.'

'If I come,' she said. 'If I come with you, I will be at the station before the train leaves.'

'How will you get there?' I asked, and hope and excitement rushed over me again.

'I will get there,' she said. 'I will get there before you. But if I am not there, then do not wait, do not come back for me. Go on your way. It will mean I do not want to come. Or I will be there.'

'But are you sure?'

'Don't stand near me now. Don't speak to me unless you have to.' She squeezed my fingers, then drew her hand away. I sauntered over to the next window, then back into the centre of the room. A gust of wind blew through a cracked window-pane and put out the candle near the couch.

'Damn the wind,' said Miss Deeds.

◆

The window in my room had burst open during the night, and there were leaves and branches strewn about the floor. I sat down on the damp bed, and smelt eucalyptus. The earth was red, as though the storm had bled it all night.

After a little while, I went into the verandah with my suitcase, to wait for the tonga. It was then that I saw Kiran under the trees. Kiran's long black pigtails were tied up in a red ribbon, and she looked fresh and clean like the rain and the red earth. She stood looking seriously at me.

'Did you like the storm?' she asked.

'Some of the time,' I said. 'I'm going soon. Can I do anything for you?'

'Where are you going?'

'I'm going to the end of the world. I'm looking for Major Roberts, have you seen him anywhere?'

'There is no Major Roberts,' she said perceptively. 'Can I come with you to the end of the world?'

'What about your parents?'

'Oh, we won't take them.'

'They might be annoyed if you go off on your own.'

'I can stay on my own. I can go anywhere.'

'Well, one day I'll come back here and I'll take you everywhere and no one will stop us. Now is there anything else I can do for you?'

'I want some flowers, but I can't reach them,' she pointed to a hibiscus tree that grew against the wall. It meant climbing the wall to reach the flowers. Some of the red flowers had fallen during the night and were floating in a pool of water.

'Alright,' I said and pulled myself up on the wall. I smiled down into Kiran's serious upturned face. 'I'll throw them to you and you can catch them.'

I bent a branch, but the wood was young and green, and I

had to twist it several times before it snapped.

'I hope nobody minds,' I said, as I dropped the flowering branch to Kiran.

'It's nobody's tree,' she said.

'Sure?'

She nodded vigorously. 'Sure, don't worry.'

I was working for her and she felt immensely capable of protecting me. Talking and being with Kiran, I felt a nostalgic longing for the childhood: emotions that had been beautiful because they were never completely understood.

'Who is your best friend?' I said.

'Daya Ram,' she replied. 'I told you so before.'

She was certainly faithful to her friends.

'And who is the second best?'

She put her finger in her mouth to consider the question; her head dropped sideways in concentration.

'I'll make you the second best,' she said.

I dropped the flowers over her head. 'That is so kind of you. I'm proud to be your second best.'

I heard the tonga bell, and from my perch on the wall saw the carriage coming down the driveway. 'That's for me,' I said. 'I must go now.'

I jumped down the wall. And the sole of my shoe came off at last.

'I knew that would happen,' I said.

'Who cares for shoes,' said Kiran.

'Who cares,' I said.

I walked back to the verandah, and Kiran walked beside me, and stood in front of the hotel while I put my suitcase in the tonga.

'You nearly stayed one day too late,' said the tonga-driver. 'Half the hotel has come down, and tonight the other half will come down.'

I climbed into the back seat. Kiran stood on the path, gazing intently at me.

'I'll see you again,' I said.

'I'll see you in Iceland or Japan,' she said. 'I'm going everywhere.'

'Maybe,' I said, 'maybe you will.'

We smiled, knowing and understanding each other's importance. In her bright eyes I saw something old and wise. The tonga-driver cracked his whip, the wheels cracked, the carriage rattled down the path. We kept waving to each other. In Kiran's hand was a spring of hibiscus. As she waved, the blossoms fell apart and danced a little in the breeze.

◆

Shamli station looked the same as it had the day before. The same train stood at the same platform, and the same dogs prowled beside the fence. I waited on the platform until the bell clanged for the train to leave, but Sushila did not come.

Somehow, I was not disappointed. I had never really expected her to come. Unattainable, Sushila would always be more bewitching and beautiful than if she were mine.

Shamli would always be there. And I could always come back, looking for Major Roberts.

MASTERJI

I was strolling along the platform, waiting for the arrival of the Amritsar Express, when I saw Mr Khushal, handcuffed to a policeman.

I hadn't recognized him at first—a paunchy gentleman with a lot of grey in his beard and a certain arrogant amusement in his manner. It was only when I came closer, and we were almost face to face, that I recognized my old Hindi teacher.

Startled, I stopped and stared. And he stared back at me, a glimmer of recognition in his eyes. It was over twenty years since I'd last seen him, standing jauntily before the classroom blackboard, and now here he was tethered to a policeman and looking as jaunty as ever...

'Good—good evening, sir,' I stammered, in my best public school manner. (You must always respect your teacher, no matter what the circumstances.)

Mr Khushal's face lit up with pleasure. 'So you remember me! It's nice to see you again, my boy.'

Forgetting that his right hand was shackled to the policeman's left, I made as if to shake hands. Mr Khushal thoughtfully took my right hand in his left and gave it a rough squeeze. A faint odour of cloves and cinnamon reached me, and I remembered how he had always been redolent of spices when standing beside my desk, watching me agonize over my Hindi–English translation.

He had joined the school in 1948, not long after the Partition. Until then there had been no Hindi teacher; we'd been taught Urdu and French. Then came a ruling that Hindi was to be a compulsory subject, and at the age of sixteen I found myself struggling with a new script. When Mr Khushal joined the staff (on the recommendation of a local official), there was no one else in the school who knew Hindi, or who could assess Mr Khushal's abilities as a teacher…

And now once again he stood before me, only this time he was in the custody of the law.

I was still recovering from the shock when the train drew in, and everyone on the platform began making a rush for the compartment doors. As the policeman elbowed his way through the crowd, I kept close behind him and his charge, and as a result I managed to get into the same third-class compartment. I found a seat right opposite Mr Khushal. He did not seem to be the least bit embarrassed by the handcuffs, or by the stares of his fellow passengers. Rather, it was the policeman who looked unhappy and ill at ease.

As the train got under way, I offered Mr Khushal one of the parathas made for me by my Ferozepur landlady. He accepted it with alacrity. I offered one to the constable as well, but although he looked at it with undisguised longing, he felt duty-bound to decline.

'Why have they arrested you, sir?' I asked. 'Is it very serious?'

'A trivial matter,' said Mr Khushal. 'Nothing to worry about. I shall be at liberty soon.'

'But what did you *do*?'

Mr Khushal leant forward. 'Nothing to be ashamed of,' he said in a confiding tone. 'Even a great teacher like Socrates fell foul of the law.'

'You mean—one of your pupils—made a complaint?'

'And why should one of my pupils make a complaint?' Mr Khushal looked offended. 'They were the beneficiaries—it was for *them*.' He noticed that I looked mystified, and decided to come straight to the point: 'It was simply a question of false certificates.'

'Oh,' I said, feeling deflated. Public school boys are always prone to jump to the wrong conclusions...

'*Your* certificates, sir?'

'Of course not. Nothing wrong with my certificates—I had them printed in Lahore, in 1946.'

'With age comes respectability,' I remarked. 'In that case, whose...?'

'Why, the matriculation certificates I've been providing all these years to the poor idiots who would never have got through on their own!'

'You mean you gave them your own certificates?'

'That's right. And if it hadn't been for so many printing mistakes, no one would have been any wiser. You can't find a good press these days, that's the trouble... It was a public service, my boy, I hope you appreciate that... It isn't fair to hold a boy back in life simply because he can't get through some puny exam... Mind you, I don't give my certificates to *anyone.* They come to me only after they have failed two or three times.'

'And I suppose you charge something?'

'Only if they can pay. There's no fixed sum. Whatever they like to give me. I've never been greedy in these matters, and you know I am not unkind...'

Which is true enough, I thought, looking out of the carriage window at the green fields of Moga and remembering the half-yearly Hindi exam when I had stared blankly at the question paper, knowing that I was totally incapable of answering any of it. Mr Khushal had come walking down the line of desks and stopped at mine, breathing cloves all over me. 'Come on, boy, why haven't you started?'

'Can't do it, sir,' I'd said. 'It's too difficult.'

'Never mind,' he'd urged in a whisper. 'Do *something.* Copy it out, copy it out!'

And so, to pass the time, I'd copied out the entire paper, word for word. And a fortnight later, when the results were out, I found I had passed!

'But, sir,' I had stammered, approaching Mr Khushal when I found him alone. 'I never answered the paper. I couldn't translate the passage. All I did was copy it out!'

'That's why I gave you pass marks,' he'd answered imperturbably. 'You have such neat handwriting. If ever you do learn Hindi, my boy, you'll write a beautiful script!'

And remembering that moment, I was now filled with compassion for my old teacher; and leaning across, I placed my hand on his knee and said: 'Sir, if they convict you, I hope it won't be for long. And when you come out, if you happen to be in Delhi or Ferozepur, please look me up. You see, I'm still rather hopeless at Hindi, and perhaps you could give me tuition. I'd be glad to pay…'

Mr Khushal threw back his head and laughed, and the entire compartment shook with his laughter.

'Teach you Hindi!' he cried. 'My dear boy, what gave you the idea that I ever knew any Hindi?'

'But, sir—if not Hindi what were you teaching us all the time at school?'

'Punjabi!' he shouted, and everyone jumped in their seats. 'Pure Punjabi! But how were *you* to know the difference?'

THE BLUE UMBRELLA

1

'Neelu! Neelu!' cried Binya.

She scrambled barefoot over the rocks, ran over the short summer grass, up and over the brow of the hill, all the time calling 'Neelu, Neelu!'

Neelu—Blue—was the name of the blue-grey cow. The other cow, which was white, was called Gori, meaning Fair One. They were fond of wandering off on their own, down to the stream or into the pine forest, and sometimes they came back by themselves and sometimes they stayed away—almost deliberately, it seemed to Binya.

If the cows didn't come home at the right time, Binya would be sent to fetch them. Sometimes her brother, Bijju, went with her, but these days he was busy preparing for his exams and didn't have time to help with the cows.

Binya liked being on her own, and sometimes she allowed the cows to lead her into some distant valley, and then they would all be late coming home. The cows preferred having Binya with them, because she let them wander. Bijju pulled them by their tails if they went too far.

Binya belonged to the mountains, to this part of the Himalayas known as Garhwal. Dark forests and lonely hilltops held no terrors for her. It was only when she was in the market town, jostled by the crowds in the bazaar, that she felt rather nervous and lost.

The town, five miles from the village, was also a pleasure resort for tourists from all over India.

Binya was probably ten. She may have been nine or even eleven, she couldn't be sure because no one in the village kept birthdays; but her mother told her she'd been born during a winter when the snow had come up to the windows, and that was just over ten years ago, wasn't it? Two years later, her father had died, but his passing had made no difference to their way of life. They had three tiny terraced fields on the side of the mountain, and they grew potatoes, onions, ginger, beans, mustard and maize: not enough to sell in the town, but enough to live on.

Like most mountain girls, Binya was quite sturdy, fair of skin, with pink cheeks and dark eyes and her black hair tied in a pigtail. She wore pretty glass bangles on her wrists, and a necklace of glass beads. From the necklace hung a leopard's claw. It was a lucky charm, and Binya always wore it. Bijju had one, too; only his was attached to a string.

Binya's full name was Binyadevi, and Bijju's real name was Vijay, but everyone called them Binya and Bijju. Binya was two years younger than her brother.

She had stopped calling for Neelu; she had heard the cowbells tinkling, and knew the cows hadn't gone far. Singing to herself, she walked over fallen pine needles into the forest glade on the spur of the hill. She heard voices, laughter, the clatter of plates and cups, and stepping through the trees, she came upon a party of picnickers.

They were holiday-makers from the plains. The women were dressed in bright saris, the men wore light summer shirts, and the children had pretty new clothes. Binya, standing in the shadows between the trees, went unnoticed; for some time she watched the picnickers, admiring their clothes, listening to their unfamiliar accents, and gazing rather hungrily at the sight of all their food.

And then her gaze came to rest on a bright blue umbrella, a frilly thing for women, which lay open on the grass beside its owner.

Now Binya had seen umbrellas before, and her mother had a big black umbrella which nobody used any more because the field rats had eaten holes in it, but this was the first time Binya had seen such a small, dainty, colourful umbrella and she fell in love with it. The umbrella was like a flower, a great blue flower that had sprung up on the dry brown hillside.

She moved forward a few paces so that she could see the umbrella better. As she came out of the shadows into the sunlight, the picnickers saw her.

'Hello, look who's here!' exclaimed the older of the two women. 'A little village girl!'

'Isn't she pretty?' remarked the other. 'But how torn and dirty her clothes are!' It did not seem to bother them that Binya could hear and understand everything they said about her.

'They're very poor in the hills,' said one of the men.

'Then let's give her something to eat.' And the older woman beckoned to Binya to come closer.

Hesitantly, nervously, Binya approached the group. Normally she would have turned and fled, but the attraction was the pretty blue umbrella. It had cast a spell over her, drawing her forward almost against her will.

'What's that on her neck?' asked the younger woman.

'A necklace of sorts.'

'It's a pendant—see, there's a claw hanging from it!'

'It's a tiger's claw,' said the man beside her. (He had never seen a tiger's claw.) 'A lucky charm. These people wear them to keep away evil spirits.' He looked to Binya for confirmation, but Binya said nothing.

'Oh, I want one too!' said the woman, who was obviously his wife.

'You can't get them in shops.'

'Buy hers, then. Give her two or three rupees, she's sure to need the money.'

The man, looking slightly embarrassed but anxious to please his young wife, produced a two-rupee note and offered it to Binya, indicating that he wanted the pendant in exchange. Binya put her hand to the necklace, half afraid that the excited woman would snatch it away from her. Solemnly she shook her head. The man then showed her a five-rupee note, but again Binya shook her head.

'How silly she is!' exclaimed the young woman.

'It may not be hers to sell,' said the man. 'But I'll try again. How much do you want—what can we give you?' And he waved his hand towards the picnic things scattered about on the grass.

Without any hesitation Binya pointed to the umbrella.

'My umbrella!' exclaimed the young woman. 'She wants my umbrella. What cheek!'

'Well, you want her pendant, don't you?'

'That's different.'

'Is it?'

The man and his wife were beginning to quarrel with each other.

'I'll ask her to go away,' said the older woman. 'We're making such fools of ourselves.'

'But I want the pendant!' cried the other, petulantly. And then, on an impulse, she picked up the umbrella and held it out to Binya. 'Here, take the umbrella!'

Binya removed her necklace and held it out to the young woman, who immediately placed it around her own neck. Then Binya took the umbrella and held it up. It did not look so small in her hands; in fact, it was just the right size.

She had forgotten about the picnickers, who were busy examining the pendant. She turned the blue umbrella this way and that, looked through the bright blue silk at the pulsating sun, and then, still keeping it open, turned and disappeared into the forest glade.

2

Binya seldom closed the blue umbrella. Even when she had it in the house, she left it lying open in a corner of the room. Sometimes Bijju snapped it shut, complaining that it got in the way. She would open it again a little later. It wasn't beautiful when it was closed.

Whenever Binya went out—whether it was to graze the cows, or fetch water from the spring, or carry milk to the little tea shop on the Tehri road—she took the umbrella with her. That patch of sky-blue silk could always be seen on the hillside.

Old Ram Bharosa (Ram the Trustworthy) kept the tea shop on the Tehri road. It was a dusty, unmetalled road. Once a day, the Tehri bus stopped near his shop and passengers got down to sip hot tea or drink a glass of buttermilk. He kept a few bottles of Coca-Cola too, but as there was no ice, the bottles got hot in the sun and so were seldom opened. He also kept sweets and toffees, and when Binya or Bijju had a few coins to spare, they would spend them at the shop. It was only a mile from the village.

Ram Bharosa was astonished to see Binya's blue umbrella.

'What have you there, Binya?' he asked.

Binya gave the umbrella a twirl and smiled at Ram Bharosa. She was always ready with her smile, and would willingly have lent it to anyone who was feeling unhappy.

'That's a lady's umbrella,' said Ram Bharosa. 'That's only for memsahibs. Where did you get it?'

'Someone gave it to me—for my necklace.'

'You exchanged it for your lucky claw!'

Binya nodded.

'But what do you need it for? The sun isn't hot enough, and it isn't meant for the rain. It's just a pretty thing for rich ladies to play with!'

Binya nodded and smiled again. Ram Bharosa was quite right; it was just a beautiful plaything. And that was exactly why she had fallen in love with it.

'I have an idea,' said the shopkeeper. 'It's no use to you, that umbrella. Why not sell it to me? I'll give you five rupees for it.'

'It's worth fifteen,' said Binya.

'Well, then, I'll give you ten.'

Binya laughed and shook her head.

'Twelve rupees?' said Ram Bharosa, but without much hope.

Binya placed a five-paise coin on the counter. 'I came for a toffee,' she said.

Ram Bharosa pulled at his drooping whiskers, gave Binya a wry look, and placed a toffee in the palm of her hand. He watched Binya as she walked away along the dusty road. The blue umbrella held him fascinated, and he stared after it until it was out of sight.

The villagers used this road to go to the market town. Some used the bus, a few rode on mules and most people walked. Today, everyone on the road turned their heads to stare at the girl with the bright blue umbrella.

Binya sat down in the shade of a pine tree. The umbrella, still open, lay beside her. She cradled her head in her arms, and presently she dozed off. It was that kind of day, sleepily warm and summery.

And while she slept, a wind sprang up.

It came quietly, swishing gently through the trees, humming softly. Then it was joined by other random gusts, bustling over the tops of the mountains. The trees shook their heads and came to life. The wind fanned Binya's cheeks. The umbrella stirred on the grass.

The wind grew stronger, picking up dead leaves and sending them spinning and swirling through the air. It got into the umbrella and began to drag it over the grass. Suddenly it lifted the umbrella and carried it about six feet from the sleeping girl. The sound woke Binya.

She was on her feet immediately, and then she was leaping down the steep slope. But just as she was within reach of the umbrella, the wind picked it up again and carried it further downhill.

Binya set off in pursuit. The wind was in a wicked, playful mood. It would leave the umbrella alone for a few moments but as soon as Binya came near, it would pick up the umbrella again and send it bouncing, floating, dancing away from her.

The hill grew steeper. Binya knew that after twenty yards it would fall away in a precipice. She ran faster. And the wind ran with her, ahead of her, and the blue umbrella stayed up with the wind.

A fresh gust picked it up and carried it to the very edge of the cliff. There it balanced for a few seconds, before toppling over, out of sight.

Binya ran to the edge of the cliff. Going down on her hands and knees, she peered down the cliff face. About a hundred feet below, a small stream rushed between great boulders. Hardly anything grew on the cliff face—just a few stunted bushes, and, halfway down, a wild cherry tree growing crookedly out of the rocks and hanging across the chasm. The umbrella had stuck in the cherry tree.

Binya didn't hesitate. She may have been timid with strangers, but she was at home on a hillside. She stuck her bare leg over the edge of the cliff and began climbing down. She kept her face to the hillside, feeling her way with her feet, only changing her handhold when she knew her feet were secure. Sometimes she held on to the thorny bilberry bushes, but she did not trust the other plants which came away very easily.

Loose stones rattled down the cliff. Once on their way, the stones did not stop until they reached the bottom of the hill; and they took other stones with them, so that there was soon a cascade of stones, and Binya had to be very careful not to start a landslide.

As agile as a mountain goat, she did not take more than five minutes to reach the crooked cherry tree. But the most difficult task remained—she had to crawl along the trunk of the tree, which stood out at right angles from the cliff. Only by doing this could she reach the trapped umbrella.

Binya felt no fear when climbing trees. She was proud of the fact that she could climb them as well as Bijju. Gripping the rough cherry bark with her toes, and using her knees as leverage, she crawled along the trunk of the projecting tree until she was almost within reach of the umbrella. She noticed with dismay that the blue cloth was torn in a couple of places.

She looked down, and it was only then that she felt afraid. She was right over the chasm, balanced precariously about eighty feet above the boulder-strewn stream. Looking down, she felt quite dizzy. Her hands shook, and the tree shook too. If she slipped now, there was only one direction in which she could fall—down, down, into the depths of that dark and shadowy ravine.

There was only one thing to do; concentrate on the patch of blue just a couple of feet away from her.

She did not look down or up, but straight ahead, and willing herself forward, she managed to reach the umbrella.

She could not crawl back with it in her hands. So, after dislodging it from the forked branch in which it had stuck, she let it fall, still open, into the ravine below. Cushioned by the wind, the umbrella floated serenely downwards, landing in a thicket of nettles.

Binya crawled back along the trunk of the cherry tree.

Twenty minutes later, she emerged from the nettle clump, her precious umbrella held aloft. She had nettle stings all over her legs, but she was hardly aware of the smarting. She was as immune to nettles as Bijju was to bees.

3

About four years previously, Bijju had knocked a hive out of an oak tree, and had been badly stung on the face and legs. It had been a painful experience. But now, if a bee stung him, he felt nothing at all: he had been immunized for life!

He was on his way home from school. It was two o'clock and he hadn't eaten since six in the morning. Fortunately, the Kingora bushes—the bilberries—were in fruit, and already Bijju's lips were stained purple with the juice of the wild, sour fruit.

He didn't have any money to spend at Ram Bharosa's shop, but he stopped there anyway to look at the sweets in their glass jars.

'And what will you have today?' asked Ram Bharosa.

'No money,' said Bijju.

'You can pay me later.'

Bijju shook his head. Some of his friends had taken sweets on credit, and at the end of the month they had found they'd eaten more sweets than they could possibly pay for! As a result, they'd had to hand over to Ram Bharosa some of their most treasured possessions—such as a curved knife for cutting grass, or a small hand-axe, or a jar for pickles, or a pair of earrings—and these had become the shopkeeper's possessions and were kept by him or sold in his shop.

Ram Bharosa had set his heart on having Binya's blue umbrella, and so naturally he was anxious to give credit to either of the children, but so far neither had fallen into the trap.

Bijju moved on, his mouth full of Kingora berries. Halfway

home, he saw Binya with the cows. It was late evening, and the sun had gone down, but Binya still had the umbrella open. The two small rents had been stitched up by her mother.

Bijju gave his sister a handful of berries. She handed him the umbrella while she ate the berries.

'You can have the umbrella until we get home,' she said. It was her way of rewarding Bijju for bringing her the wild fruit.

Calling 'Neelu! Gori!' Binya and Bijju set out for home, followed at some distance by the cows.

It was dark before they reached the village, but Bijju still had the umbrella open.

◆

Most of the people in the village were a little envious of Binya's blue umbrella. No one else had ever possessed one like it. The schoolmaster's wife thought it was quite wrong for a poor cultivator's daughter to have such a fine umbrella while she, a second-class B.A., had to make do with an ordinary black one. Her husband offered to have their old umbrella dyed blue; she gave him a scornful look, and loved him a little less than before. The pujari, who looked after the temple, announced that he would buy a multicoloured umbrella the next time he was in the town. A few days later he returned looking annoyed and grumbling that they weren't available except in Delhi. Most people consoled themselves by saying that Binya's pretty umbrella wouldn't keep out the rain, if it rained heavily; that it would shrivel in the sun, if the sun was fierce; that it would collapse in a wind, if the wind was strong; that it would attract lightning, if lightning fell near it; and that it would prove unlucky, if there was any ill luck going about. Secretly, everyone admired it.

Unlike the adults, the children didn't have to pretend. They were full of praise for the umbrella. It was so light, so pretty, so bright a blue! And it was just the right size for Binya. They knew that if they said nice things about the umbrella, Binya would smile and give it to them to hold for a little while—just a very little while!

Soon it was the time of the monsoon. Big black clouds kept piling up, and thunder rolled over the hills.

Binya sat on the hillside all afternoon, waiting for the rain. As soon as the first big drop of rain came down, she raised the umbrella over her head. More drops, big ones, came pattering down. She could see them through the umbrella silk, as they broke against the cloth.

And then there was a cloudburst, and it was like standing under a waterfall. The umbrella wasn't really a rain umbrella, but it held up bravely. Only Binya's feet got wet. Rods of rain fell around her in a curtain of shivered glass.

Everywhere on the hillside people were scurrying for shelter. Some made for a charcoal burner's hut, others for a mule-shed, or Ram Bharosa's shop. Binya was the only one who didn't run. This was what she'd been waiting for—rain on her umbrella—and she wasn't in a hurry to go home. She didn't mind getting her feet wet. The cows didn't mind getting wet either.

Presently she found Bijju sheltering in a cave. He would have enjoyed getting wet, but he had his school books with him and he couldn't afford to let them get spoilt. When he saw Binya, he came out of the cave and shared the umbrella. He was a head taller than his sister, so he had to hold the umbrella for her, while she held his books.

The cows had been left far behind.

'Neelu, Neelu!' called Binya.

'Gori!' called Bijju.

When their mother saw them sauntering home through the driving rain, she called out: 'Binya! Bijju! Hurry up and bring the cows in! What are you doing out there in the rain?'

'Just testing the umbrella,' said Bijju.

4

The rains set in, and the sun only made brief appearances. The hills turned a lush green. Ferns sprang up on walls and tree trunks. Giant lilies reared up like leopards from the tall grass. A white mist coiled and uncoiled as it floated up from the valley. It was a beautiful season, except for the leeches.

Every day, Binya came home with a couple of leeches fastened to the flesh of her bare legs. They fell off by themselves just as soon as they'd had their thimbleful of blood, but you didn't know they were on you until they fell off, and then, later, the skin became very sore and itchy. Some of the older people still believed that to be bled by leeches was a remedy for various ailments. Whenever Ram Bharosa had a headache, he applied a leech to his throbbing temple.

Three days of incessant rain had flooded out a number of small animals who lived in holes in the ground. Binya's mother suddenly found the roof full of field rats. She had to drive them out; they ate too much of her stored-up wheat flour and rice. Bijju liked lifting up large rocks to disturb the scorpions who were sleeping beneath. And snakes came out to bask in the sun.

Binya had just crossed the small stream at the bottom of the hill when she saw something gliding out of the bushes and coming towards her. It was a long black snake. A clatter of loose stones frightened it. Seeing the girl in its way, it rose up, hissing, prepared to strike. The forked tongue darted out, the venomous head lunged at Binya.

Binya's umbrella was open as usual. She thrust it forward, between herself and the snake, and the snake's hard snout thudded twice against the strong silk of the umbrella. The reptile then turned and slithered away over the wet rocks, disappearing into a clump of ferns.

Binya forgot about the cows and ran all the way home to tell her mother how she had been saved by the umbrella. Bijju had to put away his books and go out to fetch the cows. He carried a stout stick, in case he met with any snakes.

◆

First the summer sun, and now the endless rain, meant that the umbrella was beginning to fade a little. From a bright blue it had changed to a light blue. But it was still a pretty thing, and tougher than it looked, and Ram Bharosa still desired it. He did not want to sell it; he wanted to own it. He was probably the richest man in the area—so why shouldn't he have a blue umbrella? Not a day passed without his getting a glimpse of Binya and the umbrella; and the more he saw the umbrella, the more he wanted it.

The schools closed during the monsoon, but this didn't mean that Bijju could sit at home doing nothing. Neelu and Gori were providing more milk than was required at home, so Binya's mother was able to sell a kilo of milk every day: half a kilo to the schoolmaster, and half a kilo (at reduced rate) to the temple pujari. Bijju had to deliver the milk every morning.

Ram Bharosa had asked Bijju to work in his shop during the holidays, but Bijju didn't have time—he had to help his mother with the ploughing and the transplanting of the rice seedlings. So Ram Bharosa employed a boy from the next village, a boy called Rajaram. He did all the washing-up, and ran various errands. He went to the same school as Bijju, but the two boys were not friends.

One day, as Binya passed the shop, twirling her blue umbrella, Rajaram noticed that his employer gave a deep sigh and began muttering to himself.

'What's the matter, Babuji?' asked the boy.

'Oh, nothing,' said Ram Bharosa. 'It's just a sickness that has come upon me. And it's all due to that girl Binya and her wretched umbrella.'

'Why, what has she done to you?'

'Refused to sell me her umbrella! There's pride for you. And I offered her ten rupees.'

'Perhaps, if you gave her twelve...'

'But it isn't new any longer. It isn't worth eight rupees now. All the same, I'd like to have it.'

'You wouldn't make a profit on it,' said Rajaram.

'It's not the profit I'm after, wretch! It's the thing itself. It's the beauty of it!'

'And what would you do with it, Babuji? You don't visit anyone—you're seldom out of your shop. Of what use would it be to you?'

'Of what use is a poppy in a cornfield? Of what use is a rainbow? Of what use are you, numbskull? Wretch! I, too, have a soul. I want the umbrella, because—because I want its beauty to be mine!'

Rajaram put the kettle on to boil, began dusting the counter, all the time muttering: 'I'm as useful as an umbrella,' and then, after a short period of intense thought, said: 'What will you give me, Babuji, if I get the umbrella for you?'

'What do you mean?' asked the old man.

'You know what I mean. What will you give me?'

'You mean to steal it, don't you, you wretch? What a delightful child you are! I'm glad you're not my son or my enemy. But look, everyone will know it has been stolen, and then how will I be able to show off with it?'

'You will have to gaze upon it in secret,' said Rajaram with a chuckle. 'Or take it into Tehri, and have it coloured red! That's your problem. But tell me, Babuji, do you want it badly enough to pay me three rupees for stealing it without being seen?'

Ram Bharosa gave the boy a long, sad look. 'You're a sharp boy,' he said. 'You'll come to a bad end. I'll give you two rupees.'

'Three,' said the boy.

'Two,' said the old man.

'You don't really want it, I can see that,' said the boy.

'Wretch!' said the old man. 'Evil one! Darkener of my doorstep! Fetch me the umbrella, and I'll give you three rupees.'

5

Binya was in the forest glade where she had first seen the umbrella. No one came there for picnics during the monsoon. The grass was always wet and the pine needles were slippery underfoot. The tall trees shut out the light, and poisonous-looking mushrooms, orange and purple, sprang up everywhere. But it was a good place for porcupines, who seemed to like the mushrooms, and Binya was searching for porcupine quills.

The hill people didn't think much of porcupine quills, but far away in southern India, the quills were valued as charms and sold at a rupee each. So Ram Bharosa paid a tenth of a rupee for each quill brought to him, and he in turn sold the quills at a profit to a trader from the plains.

Binya had already found five quills, and she knew there'd be more in the long grass. For once, she'd put her umbrella down. She had to put it aside if she was to search the ground thoroughly.

It was Rajaram's chance.

He'd been following Binya for some time, concealing himself behind trees and rocks, creeping closer whenever she became absorbed in her search. He was anxious that she should not see him and be able to recognize him later.

He waited until Binya had wandered some distance from the umbrella. Then, running forward at a crouch, he seized the open umbrella and dashed off with it.

But Rajaram had very big feet. Binya heard his heavy footsteps and turned just in time to see him as he disappeared between the trees. She cried out, dropped the porcupine quills, and gave chase.

Binya was swift and sure-footed, but Rajaram had a long stride. All the same, he made the mistake of running downhill. A long-legged person is much faster going uphill than down. Binya reached the edge of the forest glade in time to see the thief scrambling down the path to the stream. He had closed the umbrella so that it would not hinder his flight.

Binya was beginning to gain on the boy. He kept to the path, while she simply slid and leapt down the steep hillside. Near the bottom of the hill the path began to straighten out, and it was here that the long-legged boy began to forge ahead again.

Bijju was coming home from another direction. He had a bundle of sticks which he'd collected for the kitchen fire. As he reached the path, he saw Binya rushing down the hill as though all the mountain spirits in Garhwal were after her.

'What's wrong?' he called. 'Why are you running?'

Binya paused only to point at the fleeing Rajaram.

'My umbrella!' she cried. 'He has stolen it!'

Bijju dropped his bundle of sticks, and ran after his sister. When he reached her side, he said, 'I'll soon catch him!' and went sprinting away over the lush green grass. He was fresh, and he was soon well ahead of Binya and gaining on the thief.

Rajaram was crossing the shallow stream when Bijju caught up with him. Rajaram was the taller boy, but Bijju was much stronger. He flung himself at the thief, caught him by the legs, and brought him down in the water. Rajaram got to his feet and tried to drag himself away, but Bijju still had him by a leg. Rajaram overbalanced and came down with a great splash. He had let the umbrella fall. It began to float away on the current. Just then Binya arrived, flushed and breathless, and went dashing into the stream after the umbrella.

Meanwhile, a tremendous fight was taking place. Locked in fierce combat, the two boys swayed together on a rock, tumbled on to the sand, rolled over and over the pebbled bank until they were again thrashing about in the shallows of the stream. The magpies, bulbuls and other birds were disturbed, and flew away with cries of alarm.

Covered with mud, gasping and spluttering, the boys groped for each other in the water. After five minutes of frenzied struggle, Bijju emerged victorious. Rajaram lay flat on his back on the sand, exhausted, while Bijju sat astride him, pinning him down with his arms and legs.

'Let me get up!' gasped Rajaram. 'Let me go—I don't want your useless umbrella!'

'Then why did you take it?' demanded Bijju. 'Come on—tell me why!'

'It was that skinflint Ram Bharosa,' said Rajaram. 'He told me to get it for him. He said if I didn't fetch it, I'd lose my job.'

6

By early October, the rains were coming to an end. The leeches disappeared. The ferns turned yellow, and the sunlight on the green hills was mellow and golden, like the limes on the small tree in front of Binya's home. Bijju's days were happy ones as he came home from school, munching on roasted corn. Binya's umbrella had turned a pale milky blue, and was patched in several places, but it was still the prettiest umbrella in the village, and she still carried it with her wherever she went.

The cold, cruel winter wasn't far off, but somehow October seems longer than other months, because it is a kind month: the grass is good to be upon, the breeze is warm and gentle and pine-scented. That October, everyone seemed contented—everyone, that is, except Ram Bharosa.

The old man had by now given up all hope of ever possessing Binya's umbrella. He wished he had never set eyes on it. Because of the umbrella, he had suffered the tortures of greed, the despair of loneliness. Because of the umbrella, people had stopped coming to his shop!

Ever since it had become known that Ram Bharosa had tried to have the umbrella stolen, the village people had turned against him. They stopped trusting the old man, instead of buying their soap and tea and matches from his shop, they preferred to walk an extra mile to the shops near the Tehri bus stand. Who would have dealings with a man who had sold his soul for an umbrella? The children taunted him, twisted his name around. From 'Ram the Trustworthy' he became 'Trusty Umbrella Thief'.

The old man sat alone in his empty shop, listening to the eternal hissing of his kettle and wondering if anyone would ever again step in for a glass of tea. Ram Bharosa had lost his own appetite, and ate and drank very little. There was no money coming in. He had his savings in a bank in Tehri, but it was a terrible thing to have to dip into them! To save money, he had dismissed the blundering Rajaram. So he was left without any company. The roof leaked and the wind got in through the corrugated tin sheets, but Ram Bharosa didn't care.

Bijju and Binya passed his shop almost every day. Bijju went by with a loud but tuneless whistle. He was one of the world's whistlers; cares rested lightly on his shoulders. But, strangely enough, Binya crept quietly past the shop, looking the other way, almost as though she was in some way responsible for the misery of Ram Bharosa.

She kept reasoning with herself, telling herself that the umbrella was her very own, and that she couldn't help it if others were jealous of it. But had she loved the umbrella too much? Had it mattered more to her than people mattered? She couldn't help feeling that, in a small way, she was the cause of the sad look on Ram Bharosa's face ('His face is a yard long,' said Bijju) and the ruinous condition of his shop. It was all due to his own greed, no doubt, but she didn't want him to feel too bad about what he'd done, because it made her feel bad about herself; and so she closed the umbrella whenever she came near the shop, opening it again only when she was out of sight.

One day towards the end of October, when she had ten paise in her pocket, she entered the shop and asked the old man for a toffee.

She was Ram Bharosa's first customer in almost two weeks. He looked suspiciously at the girl. Had she come to taunt him, to flaunt the umbrella in his face? She had placed her coin on the counter. Perhaps it was a bad coin. Ram Bharosa picked it up and bit it; he held it up to the light; he rang it on the ground. It was a good coin. He gave Binya the toffee.

Binya had already left the shop when Ram Bharosa saw the closed umbrella lying on his counter. There it was, the blue umbrella he had always wanted, within his grasp at last! He had only to hide it at the back of his shop, and no one would know that he had it, no one could prove that Binya had left it behind.

He stretched out his trembling, bony hand, and took the umbrella by the handle. He pressed it open. He stood beneath it, in the dark shadows of his shop, where no sun or rain could ever touch it.

'But I'm never in the sun or in the rain,' he said aloud. 'Of what use is an umbrella to me?'

And he hurried outside and ran after Binya.

'Binya, Binya!' he shouted. 'Binya, you've left your umbrella behind!'

He wasn't used to running, but he caught up with her, held out the umbrella, saying, 'You forgot it—the umbrella!'

In that moment it belonged to both of them.

But Binya didn't take the umbrella. She shook her head and said, 'You keep it. I don't need it any more.'

'But it's such a pretty umbrella!' protested Ram Bharosa. 'It's the best umbrella in the village.'

'I know,' said Binya. 'But an umbrella isn't everything.'

And she left the old man holding the umbrella, and went tripping down the road, and there was nothing between her and the bright blue sky.

7

Well, now that Ram Bharosa has the blue umbrella—a gift from Binya, as he tells everyone—he is sometimes persuaded to go out into the sun or the rain, and as a result he looks much healthier. Sometimes he uses the umbrella to chase away pigs or goats. It is always left open outside the shop, and anyone who wants to borrow it may do so; and so in a way it has become everyone's umbrella. It is faded and patchy, but it is still the best umbrella in the village.

People are visiting Ram Bharosa's shop again. Whenever Bijju or Binya stop for a cup of tea, he gives them a little extra milk or sugar. They like their tea sweet and milky.

A few nights ago, a bear visited Ram Bharosa's shop. There had been snow on the higher ranges of the Himalayas, and the bear had been finding it difficult to obtain food; so it had come lower down, to see what it could pick up near the village. That night it scrambled on to the tin roof of Ram Bharosa's shop, and made off with a huge pumpkin which had been ripening on the roof. But in climbing off the roof, the bear had lost a claw.

Next morning Ram Bharosa found the claw just outside the door of his shop. He picked it up and put it in his pocket. A bear's claw was a lucky find.

A day later, when he went into the market town, he took the claw with him, and left it with a silversmith, giving the craftsman certain instructions.

The silversmith made a locket for the claw, then he gave it a thin silver chain. When Ram Bharosa came again, he paid the silversmith ten rupees for his work.

The days were growing shorter, and Binya had to be home a little earlier every evening. There was a hungry leopard at large, and she couldn't leave the cows out after dark.

She was hurrying past Ram Bharosa's shop when the old man called out to her.

'Binya, spare a minute! I want to show you something.'

Binya stepped into the shop.

'What do you think of it?' asked Ram Bharosa, showing her the silver pendant with the claw.

'It's so beautiful,' said Binya, just touching the claw and the silver chain.

'It's a bear's claw,' said Ram Bharosa. 'That's even luckier than a leopard's claw. Would you like to have it?'

'I have no money,' said Binya.

'That doesn't matter. You gave me the umbrella, I give you the claw! Come, let's see what it looks like on you.'

He placed the pendant on Binya, and indeed it looked very beautiful on her.

Ram Bharosa says he will never forget the smile she gave him when she left the shop.

She was halfway home when she realized she had left the cows behind.

'Neelu, Neelu!' she called. 'Oh, Gori!'

There was a faint tinkle of bells as the cows came slowly down the mountain path.

In the distance she could hear her mother and Bijju calling for her.

She began to sing. They heard her singing, and knew she was safe and near.

She walked home through the darkening glade, singing of the stars, and the trees stood still and listened to her, and the mountains were glad.

WILSON'S BRIDGE

The old wooden bridge has gone, and today an iron suspension bridge straddles the Bhagirathi as it rushes down the gorge below Gangotri. But villagers will tell you that you can still hear the hooves of Wilson's horse as he gallops across the bridge he had built 150 years ago. At the time people were sceptical of its safety, and so, to prove its sturdiness, he rode across it again and again. Parts of the old bridge can still be seen on the far bank of the river. And the legend of Wilson and his pretty hill bride, Gulabi, is still well known in this region.

I had joined some friends in the old forest rest house near the river. There were the Rays, recently married, and the Duttas, married many years. The younger Rays quarrelled frequently; the older Duttas looked on with more amusement than concern. I was a part of their group and yet something of an outsider. As a single man, I was a person of no importance. And as a marriage counsellor, I wouldn't have been of any use to them.

I spent most of my time wandering along the river banks or exploring the thick deodar and oak forests that covered the slopes. It was these trees that had made a fortune for Wilson and his patron, the Raja of Tehri. They had exploited the great forests to the full, floating huge logs downstream to the timber yards in the plains.

Returning to the rest house late one evening, I was halfway across the bridge when I saw a figure at the other end, emerging from the mist. Presently I made out a woman, wearing the plain dhoti of the hills; her hair fell loose over her shoulders. She appeared not to see me, and reclined against the railing of the bridge, looking down at the rushing waters far below. And then, to my amazement and horror, she climbed over the railing and threw herself into the river.

I ran forward, calling out, but I reached the railing only to see her fall into the foaming waters below, from where she was carried swiftly downstream.

The watchman's cabin stood a little way off. The door was open. The watchman, Ram Singh, was reclining on his bed, smoking a hookah.

'Someone just jumped off the bridge,' I said breathlessly. 'She's been swept down the river!'

The watchman was unperturbed. 'Gulabi again,' he said, almost to himself; and then to me, 'Did you see her clearly?'

'Yes, a woman with long loose hair—but I didn't see her face very clearly.'

'It must have been Gulabi. Only a ghost, my dear sir. Nothing to be alarmed about. Every now and then someone sees her throw herself into the river. Sit down,' he said, gesturing towards a battered old armchair, 'be comfortable and I'll tell you all about it.'

I was far from comfortable, but I listened to Ram Singh tell me the tale of Gulabi's suicide. After making me a glass of hot sweet tea, he launched into a long, rambling account of how Wilson, a British adventurer seeking his fortune, had been hunting musk deer when he encountered Gulabi on the path from her village. The girl's grey-green eyes and peach-blossom complexion enchanted him, and he went out of his way to get to know her people. Was he in love with her, or did he simply find her beautiful and desirable? We shall never really know. In the course of his travels and adventures he had known many women, but Gulabi was different, childlike and ingenuous, and he decided he would marry her. The humble family to which she belonged had no objection. Hunting had its limitations, and Wilson found it more profitable to tap the region's great forest wealth. In a few years he had made a fortune. He built a large timbered house at Harsil, another in Dehradun and a third at Mussoorie. Gulabi had all she could have wanted, including two robust little sons. When he was away on work, she looked after their children and their large apple orchard at Harsil.

And then came the evil day when Wilson met the Englishwoman, Ruth, on the Mussoorie Mall, and decided that she should have a share of his affections and his wealth. A fine house was provided for her, too. The time he spent at Harsil with Gulabi and his children dwindled. 'Business affairs'—he was now one of the owners of a bank—kept him in the fashionable hill resort. He was a popular host and took his friends and associates on shikar parties in the Doon.

Gulabi brought up her children in village style. She heard stories of Wilson's dalliance with the Mussoorie woman and, on one of his rare visits, she confronted him and voiced her resentment, demanding that he leave the other woman. He brushed her aside and told her not to listen to idle gossip. When he turned away from her, she picked up the flintlock pistol that lay on the gun table and fired one shot at him. The bullet missed him and shattered her looking glass. Gulabi ran out of the house, through the orchard and into the forest, then down the steep path to the bridge built by Wilson only two or three years before. When he had recovered his composure, he mounted his horse and came looking for her. It was too late. She had already thrown herself off the bridge into the swirling waters far below. Her body was found a mile or two downstream, caught between some rocks.

This was the tale that Ram Singh told me, with various flourishes and interpolations of his own. I thought it would make a good story to tell my friends that evening, before the fireside in the rest house. They found the story fascinating, but when I told them I had seen Gulabi's ghost, they thought I was doing a little embroidering of my own. Mrs Dutta thought it was a tragic tale. Young Mrs Ray thought Gulabi had been very silly. 'She was a simple girl,' opined Mr Dutta. 'She responded in the only way she knew...'; 'Money can't buy happiness,' said Mr Ray. 'No,' said Mrs Dutta, 'but it can buy you a great many comforts.' Mrs Ray wanted to talk of other things, so I changed the subject. It can get a little confusing for a bachelor who must spend the evening with two married couples. There are undercurrents which he is aware of but not equipped to deal with.

I would walk across the bridge quite often after that. It was busy with traffic during the day, but after dusk there were only a few vehicles on the road and seldom any pedestrians. A mist rose from the gorge below and obscured the far end of the bridge. I preferred walking there in the evening, half expecting, half hoping to see Gulabi's ghost again. It was her face that I really wanted to see. Would she still be as beautiful as she was fabled to be?

It was on the evening before our departure that something happened that would haunt me for a long time afterwards.

There was a feeling of restiveness as our days there drew to a close. The Rays had apparently made up their differences, although they weren't talking very much. Mr Dutta was anxious to get back to his office in Delhi and Mrs Dutta's rheumatism was playing up. I was restless too, wanting to return to my writing desk in Mussoorie.

That evening I decided to take one last stroll across the bridge to enjoy the cool breeze of a summer's night in the mountains. The moon hadn't come up, and it was really quite dark, although there were lamps at either end of the bridge providing sufficient light for those who wished to cross over.

I was standing in the middle of the bridge, in the darkest part, listening to the river thundering down the gorge, when I saw the sari-draped figure emerging from the lamplight and making towards the railings.

Instinctively I called out, 'Gulabi!'

She half turned towards me, but I could not see her clearly. The wind had blown her hair across her face and all I saw was wildly staring eyes. She raised herself over the railing and threw herself off the bridge. I heard the splash as her body struck the water far below.

Once again I found myself running towards the part of the railing where she had jumped. And then someone was running towards the same spot, from the direction of the rest house. It was young Mr Ray.

'My wife!' he cried out. 'Did you see my wife?'

He rushed to the railing and stared down at the swirling waters of the river.

'Look! There she is!' He pointed at a helpless figure bobbing about in the water.

We ran down the steep bank to the river but the current had swept her on. Scrambling over rocks and bushes, we made frantic efforts to catch up with the drowning woman. But the river in that defile is a roaring torrent, and it was over an hour before we were able to retrieve poor Mrs Ray's body, caught in driftwood about a mile downstream.

She was cremated not far from where we found her and we returned to our various homes in gloom and grief, chastened but none the wiser for the experience.

If you happen to be in that area and decide to cross the bridge late in the evening, you might see Gulabi's ghost or hear the hoofbeats of Wilson's horse as he canters across the old wooden bridge looking for her. Or you might see the ghost of Mrs Ray and hear her husband's anguished cry. Or there might be others. Who knows?

TORIA AND THE DAUGHTER OF THE SUN

Once upon a time there was a young shepherd of the Santal tribe named Toria, who grazed his sheep and goats on the bank of a river. Now it happened that the daughters of the Sun would descend from heaven every day by means of a spider's web, to bathe in the river. Finding Toria there, they invited him to bathe with them. After they had bathed and anointed themselves with oils and perfumes, they returned to their heavenly abode, while Toria went to look after his flock.

Having become friendly with the daughters of the Sun, Toria gradually fell in love with one of them. But he was at a loss to know how to obtain such a divine creature. One day, when they met him and said, 'Come along, Toria, and bathe with us,' he suddenly thought of a plan.

While they were bathing, he said, 'Let us see who can stay under water the longest.' At a given signal they all dived, but very soon Toria raised his head above water and, making sure that no one was looking, hurried out of the water, picked up the robe of the girl he loved, and was in the act of carrying it away when the others raised their heads above the water.

The girl ran after him, begging him to return her garment, but Toria did not stop till he had reached his home. When she arrived, he gave her the robe without a word. Seeing such a beautiful and noble creature before him, for very bashfulness he could not open his mouth to ask her to marry him; so he simply said, 'You can go now.'

But she replied, 'No, I will not return. My sisters by this time will have gone home. I will stay with you, and be your wife.'

All the time this was going on, a parrot, whom Toria had taught to speak, kept on flying about the heavens, calling out to the Sun: 'Oh, great Father, do not look downwards!' As a result, the Sun did not see what was happening on earth to his daughter.

This girl was very different from the women of the country—she was half human, half divine—so that when a beggar came to the house and saw her, his eyes were dazzled just as if he had stared at the Sun.

It happened that this same beggar in the course of his wanderings came to the king's palace, and having seen the queen, who was thought by all to be the most beautiful of women, he told the king: 'The shepherd Toria's wife is far more beautiful than your queen. If you were to see her, you would be enchanted.'

'How can I see her?' asked the king eagerly.

The beggar answered, 'Put on your old clothes and travel in disguise.'

The king did so, and having arrived at the shepherd's house, asked for alms. Toria's wife came out of the house and gave him food and water, but he was so astonished at seeing her great beauty that he was unable to eat or drink. His only thought was: How can I manage to make her my queen?

When he got home he thought over many plans and at length decided upon one. He said, 'I will order Toria to dig a large tank with his own hands, and fill it with water, and if he does not perform the task, I will kill him and seize his wife.' He then summoned Toria to the palace, commanded him to dig the tank and threatened him with death if he failed to fill the tank with water the same night.

Toria returned home slowly and sorrowfully.

'What makes you so sad today?' asked his wife.

He replied, 'The king has ordered me to dig a large tank, to fill it with water, and also to make trees grow beside it, all in the course of one night.'

'Don't let it worry you,' said his wife. 'Take your spade and mix a little water with the sand, where the tank is to be, and it will form there by itself.'

Toria did as he was told, and the king was astonished to find the tank completed in time. He had no excuse for killing Toria.

Later, the king planted a great plain with mustard seeds. When it was ready for reaping, he commanded Toria to reap and gather the produce into one large heap on a certain day; failing which, he would certainly be put to death.

Toria, hearing this, was again very sad. When he told his wife about it, she said, 'Do not worry, it will be done.' So the daughter of the Sun summoned her children, the doves. They came in large numbers, and in the space of an hour carried the produce away to the king's threshing floor. Again, Toria was saved through the wisdom of his wife. However, the king determined not to be outdone, so he arranged a great hunt. On the day of the hunt he assembled his retainers, and a large number of beaters and provision-carriers, and set out for the jungle. Toria was employed to carry eggs and water. But the object of the hunt was not to kill a tiger, it was to kill Toria, so that the king might seize the daughter of the Sun and make her his wife.

Arriving at a cave, they said that a hare had taken refuge in it. They forced Toria into the cave. Then, rolling large stones against the entrance, they completely blocked it. They gathered large quantities of brushwood at the mouth of the cave, and set fire to it to smother Toria. Having done this, they returned home, boasting that they had finally disposed of the shepherd. But Toria broke the eggs, and all the ashes were scattered. Then he poured the water that he had with him on the remaining embers, and the fire was extinguished. Toria managed to crawl out of the cave. And there, to his great astonishment, he saw that all the white ashes of the fire were becoming cows, whilst the half-burnt wood was turning into buffaloes.

Toria herded the cows and buffaloes together, and drove them home.

When the king saw the herd, he became very envious, and asked Toria where he had found such fine cows and buffaloes. Toria said, 'From that cave into which you pushed me. I did not bring many with me, being on my own. But if you and all your retainers go, you will be able to get as many as you want. But to catch them it will be necessary to close the door of the cave, and light a fire in front, as you did for me.'

'Very well,' said the king. 'I and my people will enter the cave, and, as you have sufficient cows and buffaloes, kindly do not go into the cave with us, but kindle the fire outside.'

The king and his people then entered the cave. Toria blocked up the doorway, and then lit a large fire at the entrance. Before long, all that were in the cave were suffocated.

Some days later the daughter of the Sun said, 'I want to visit my father's house.'

Toria said, 'Very well, I will also go with you.'

'No, it is foolish of you to think of such a thing,' she said. 'You will not be able to get there.'

'If you are able to go, surely I can.' And he insisted on accompanying her.

After travelling a great distance, Toria became so faint from the heat of the sun that he could go no further. His wife said, 'Did I not warn you? As for quenching your thirst, there is no water to be found here. But sit down and rest. I will see if I can find some for you.'

While she was away, driven by his great thirst, Toria sucked a raw egg that he had brought with him. No sooner had he done this than he changed into a fowl. When his wife returned with water, she could not find him anywhere; but, sitting where she had left him, was a solitary fowl. Taking the bird in her arms, she continued her journey.

When she reached her father's house, her sisters asked her, 'Where is Toria, your husband?' She replied, 'I don't know. I left him on the road while I went to fetch water. When I returned, he had disappeared. Perhaps he will turn up later.'

Her sisters, seeing the fowl, thought that it would make a good meal. And so, while Toria's wife was resting, they killed and ate the fowl. Later, when they again inquired of her as to the whereabouts of her husband, she looked thoughtful.

'I can't be sure,' she said. 'But I think you have eaten him.'

THE MONKEYS

I couldn't be sure, next morning, if I had been dreaming or if I had really heard dogs barking in the night and had seen them scampering about on the hillside below the cottage. There had been a golden Cocker, a Retriever, a Peke, a Dachshund, a black Labrador and one or two nondescripts. They had woken me with their barking shortly after midnight, and had made so much noise that I had got out of bed and looked out of the open window. I saw them quite plainly in the moonlight, five or six dogs rushing excitedly through the bracken and long monsoon grass.

It was only because there had been so many breeds among the dogs that I felt a little confused. I had been in the cottage only a week, and I was already on nodding or speaking terms with most of my neighbours. Colonel Fanshawe, retired from the Indian army, was my immediate neighbour. He did keep a Cocker, but it was black. The elderly Anglo-Indian spinsters who lived beyond the deodars kept only cats. (Though why cats should be the prerogative of spinsters, I have never been able to understand.) The milkman kept a couple of mongrels. And the Punjabi industrialist who had bought a former prince's palace—without ever occupying it—left the property in charge of a watchman who kept a huge Tibetan mastiff.

None of these dogs looked like the ones I had seen in the night.

'Does anyone here keep a Retriever?' I asked Colonel Fanshawe, when I met him taking his evening walk.

'No one that I know of,' he said and gave me a swift, penetrating look from under his bushy eyebrows. 'Why, have you seen one around?'

'No, I just wondered. There are a lot of dogs in the area, aren't there?'

'Oh, yes. Nearly everyone keeps a dog here. Of course, every now and then a panther carries one off. Lost a lovely little terrier myself only last winter.'

Colonel Fanshawe, tall and red-faced, seemed to be waiting for me to tell him something more—or was he just taking time to recover his breath after a stiff uphill climb?

That night I heard the dogs again. I went to the window and looked out. The moon was at the full, silvering the leaves of the oak trees.

The dogs were looking up into the trees and barking. But I could see nothing in the trees, not even an owl.

I gave a shout, and the dogs disappeared into the forest.

Colonel Fanshawe looked at me expectantly when I met him the following day. He knew something about those dogs, of that I was certain; but he was waiting to hear what I had to say. I decided to oblige him.

'I saw at least six dogs in the middle of the night,' I said. 'A Cocker, a Retriever, a Peke, a Dachshund and two mongrels. Now, Colonel, I'm sure you must know whose they are.'

The Colonel was delighted. I could tell by the way his eyes glinted that he was going to enjoy himself at my expense.

'You've been seeing Miss Fairchild's dogs,' he said with smug satisfaction.

'Oh, and where does she live?'

'She doesn't, my boy. Died fifteen years ago.'

'Then what are her dogs doing here?'

'Looking for monkeys,' said the Colonel. And he stood back to watch my reaction.

'I'm afraid I don't understand,' I said.

'Let me put it this way,' said the Colonel. 'Do you believe in ghosts?'

'I've never seen any,' I said.

'But you have, my boy, you have. Miss Fairchild's dogs died years ago—a Cocker, a Retriever, a Dachshund, a Peke and two mongrels. They were buried on a little knoll under the oaks. Nothing odd about their deaths, mind you. They were all quite old, and didn't survive their mistress very long. Neighbours looked after them until they died.'

'And Miss Fairchild lived in the cottage where I stay? Was she young?'

'She was in her mid-forties, an athletic sort of woman, fond of the outdoors. Didn't care much for men. I thought you knew about her.'

'No, I haven't been here very long, you know. But what was it you said about monkeys? Why were the dogs looking for monkeys?'

'Ah, that's the interesting part of the story. Have you seen the langur monkeys that sometimes come to eat oak leaves?'

'No.'

'You will, sooner or later. There has always been a band of them roaming these forests. They're quite harmless really, except that they'll ruin a garden if given half a chance… Well, Miss Fairchild fairly loathed those monkeys. She was very keen on her dahlias—grew some prize specimens—but the monkeys would come at night, dig up the plants and eat the dahlia bulbs. Apparently they found the bulbs much to their liking. Miss Fairchild would be furious. People who are passionately fond of gardening often go off balance when their best plants are ruined—that's only human, I suppose. Miss Fairchild set her dogs on the monkeys whenever she could, even if it was in the middle of the night. But the monkeys simply took to the trees and left the dogs barking.

'Then one day—or rather one night—Miss Fairchild took desperate measures. She borrowed a shotgun and sat up near a window. And when the monkeys arrived, she shot one of them dead.'

The Colonel paused and looked out over the oak trees which were shimmering in the warm afternoon sun.

'She shouldn't have done that,' he said.

'Never shoot a monkey. It's not only that they're sacred to Hindus—but they are rather human, you know. Well, I must be getting on. Good day!' And the Colonel, having ended his story rather abruptly, set off at a brisk pace through the deodars.

I didn't hear the dogs that night. But the next day I saw the monkeys—the real ones, not ghosts. There were about twenty of them, young and old, sitting in the trees munching oak leaves. They didn't pay much attention to me, and I watched them for some time.

They were handsome creatures, their fur a silver-grey, their tails long and sinuous. They leapt gracefully from tree to tree, and were very polite and dignified in their behaviour towards each other—unlike the bold, rather crude red monkeys of the plains. Some of the younger ones scampered about on the hillside, playing and wrestling with each other like schoolboys.

There were no dogs to molest them—and no dahlias to tempt them into the garden.

But that night, I heard the dogs again. They were barking more furiously than ever.

'Well, I'm not getting up for them this time,' I mumbled, and pulled the blanket over my ears.

But the barking grew louder, and was joined by other sounds, a squealing and a scuffling.

Then suddenly, the piercing shriek of a woman rang through the forest. It was an unearthly sound, and it made my hair stand up.

I leapt out of bed and dashed to the window.

A woman was lying on the ground, three or four huge monkeys were on top of her, biting her arms and pulling at her throat. The dogs were yelping and trying to drag the monkeys off, but they were being harried from behind by others. The woman gave another bloodcurdling shriek, and I dashed back into the room, grabbed hold of a small axe and ran into the garden.

But everyone—dogs, monkeys and shrieking woman—had disappeared, and I stood alone on the hillside in my pyjamas, clutching an axe and feeling very foolish.

The Colonel greeted me effusively the following day.

'Still seeing those dogs?' he asked in a bantering tone.

'I've seen the monkeys too,' I said.

'Oh, yes, they've come around again. But they're real enough, and quite harmless.'

'I know—but I saw them last night with the dogs.'

'Oh, did you really? That's strange, very strange.'

The Colonel tried to avoid my eye, but I hadn't quite finished with him.

'Colonel,' I said. 'You never did get around to telling me how Miss Fairchild died.'

'Oh, didn't I? Must have slipped my memory. I'm getting old, don't remember people as well as I used to. But, of course, I remember about Miss Fairchild, poor lady. The monkeys killed her. Didn't you know? They simply tore her to pieces...'

His voice trailed off, and he looked thoughtfully at a caterpillar that was making its way up his walking stick.

'She shouldn't have shot one of them,' he said. 'Never shoot a monkey—they're rather human, you know...'

THE PLAYING FIELDS OF SIMLA

It had been a lonely winter for a twelve-year-old boy. I hadn't really got over my father's untimely death two years previously; nor had I as yet reconciled myself to my mother's marriage to the Punjabi gentleman who dealt in second-hand cars. The three-month winter break over, I was almost happy to return to my boarding school in Simla—that elegant hill station once celebrated by Kipling and soon to lose its status as the summer capital of the Raj in India.

It wasn't as though I had many friends at school. I had always been a bit of a loner, shy and reserved, looking out only for my father's rare visits—on his brief leaves from RAF duties—and to my sharing his tent or air force hutment outside Delhi or Karachi. Those unsettled but happy days would not come again. I needed a friend but it was not easy to find one among a horde of rowdy, pea-shooting fourth formers, who carved their names on desks and stuck chewing gum on the class teacher's chair. Had I grown up with other children, I might have developed a taste for schoolboy anarchy; but, in sharing my father's loneliness after his separation from my mother, I had turned into a premature adult. The mixed nature of my reading—Dickens, Richmal Crompton, Tagore and *Champion* and *Film Fun* comics—probably reflected the confused state of my life. A book reader was rare even in those pre-electronic times. On rainy days most boys played cards or Monopoly, or listened to Artie Shaw on the wind-up gramophone in the common room.

After a month in the fourth form I began to notice a new boy, Omar, and then only because he was a quiet, almost taciturn person who took no part in the form's feverish attempts to imitate the Marx Brothers at the circus. He showed no resentment at the prevailing anarchy, nor did he make a move to participate in it. Once he caught me looking at him, and he smiled ruefully, tolerantly. Did I sense another adult in the class? Someone who was a little older than his years?

Even before we began talking to each other, Omar and I developed an understanding of sorts, and we'd nod almost respectfully to each other when we met in the classroom corridors or the environs of the dining hall or dormitory. We were not in the same house. The house system practised its own form of apartheid, whereby a member of, say, Curzon House was not expected to fraternize with someone belonging to Rivaz or Lefroy! Those public schools certainly knew how to clamp you into compartments. However, these barriers vanished when Omar and I found ourselves selected for the School Colts' hockey team—Omar as a fullback, I as goalkeeper. I think a defensive position suited me by nature. In all modesty I have to say that I made a good goalkeeper, both at hockey and football. And fifty years on, I am still keeping goal. Then I did it between goalposts, now I do it off the field—protecting a family, protecting my independence as a writer…

The taciturn Omar now spoke to me occasionally, and we combined well on the field of play. A good understanding is needed between goalkeeper and fullback. We were on the same wavelength. I anticipated his moves, he was familiar with mine. Years later, when I read Conrad's *The Secret Sharer*, I thought of Omar.

It wasn't until we were away from the confines of school, classroom and dining hall that our friendship flourished. The hockey team travelled to Sanawar on the next mountain range, where we were to play a couple of matches against our old rivals, the Lawrence Royal Military School. This had been my father's old school, but I did not know that in his time it had also been a military orphanage. Grandfather, who had been a private foot soldier—of the likes of Kipling's Mulvaney, Otheris and Learoyd—had joined the Scottish Rifles after leaving home at the age of seventeen. He had died while his children were still very young, but my father's more rounded education had enabled him to become an officer.

Omar and I were thrown together a good deal during the visit to Sanawar, and in our more leisurely moments, strolling undisturbed around a school where we were guests and not pupils, we exchanged life histories and other confidences. Omar, too, had lost his father—had I sensed that before?—shot in some tribal encounter on the Frontier, for he hailed from the lawless lands beyond Peshawar. A wealthy uncle was seeing to Omar's education. The RAF was now seeing to mine.

We wandered into the school chapel, and there I found my father's name—A.A. Bond—on the school's roll of honour board: old boys who had lost their lives while serving during the two World Wars.

'What did his initials stand for?' asked Omar.

'Aubrey Alexander.'

'Unusual names, like yours. Why did your parents call you Ruskin?'

'I am not sure. I think my father liked the works of John Ruskin, who wrote on serious subjects like art and architecture. I don't think anyone reads him now. They'll read me, though!' I had already started writing my first book. It was called *Nine Months* (the length of the school term, not a pregnancy), and it described some of the happenings at school and lampooned a few of our teachers. I had filled three slim exercise books with this premature literary project, and I allowed Omar to go through them. He must have been my first reader and critic. 'They're very interesting,' he said, 'but you'll get into trouble if someone finds them. Especially Mr Oliver.' And he read out an offending verse:

Olly, Olly, Olly, with his balls on a trolley,
And his arse all painted green!

I have to admit it wasn't great literature. I was better at hockey and football. I made some spectacular saves, and we won our matches against Sanawar. When we returned to Simla, we were school heroes for a couple of days and lost some of our reticence; we were even a little more forthcoming with other boys. And then Mr Fisher, my housemaster, discovered my literary opus, *Nine Months,* under my mattress, and took it away and read it (as he told me later) from cover to cover. Corporal punishment then being in vogue, I was given six of the best with a springy malacca cane, and my manuscript was torn up and deposited in Fisher's waste-paper basket. All I had to show for my efforts were some purple welts on my bottom. These were proudly displayed to all who were interested, and I was a hero for another two days.

'Will you go away too when the British leave India?' Omar asked me one day.

'I don't think so,' I said. 'My stepfather is Indian.'

'Everyone is saying that our leaders and the British are going to divide the country. Simla will be in India, Peshawar in Pakistan!'

'Oh, it won't happen,' I said glibly. 'How can they cut up such a big country?' But even as we chatted about the possibility, Nehru and Jinnah and Mountbatten and all those who mattered were preparing their instruments for major surgery.

Before their decision impinged on our lives and everyone else's, we found a little freedom of our own—in an underground tunnel that we discovered below the third flat.

It was really part of an old, disused drainage system, and when Omar and I began exploring it, we had no idea just how far it extended. After crawling along on our bellies for some twenty feet, we found ourselves in complete darkness. Omar had brought along a small pencil torch, and with its help we continued writhing forward (moving backwards would have been quite impossible) until we saw a glimmer of light at the end of the tunnel. Dusty, musty, very scruffy, we emerged at last on to a grassy knoll, a little way outside the school boundary.

It's always a great thrill to escape beyond the boundaries that adults have devised. Here we were in unknown territory. To travel without passports—that would be the ultimate in freedom!

But more passports were on their way and more boundaries.

Lord Mountbatten, viceroy and governor-general-to-be, came for our Founder's Day and gave away the prizes. I had won a prize for something or the other, and mounted the rostrum to receive my book from this towering, handsome man in his pinstripe suit. Bishop Cotton's was then the premier school of India, often referred to as the 'Eton of the East'. Viceroys and governors had graced its functions. Many of its boys had gone on to eminence in the civil services and armed forces. There was one 'old boy' about whom they maintained a stolid silence—General Dyer, who had ordered the massacre at Amritsar and destroyed the trust that had been building up between Britain and India.

Now Mountbatten spoke of the momentous events that were happening all around us—the War had just come to an end, the United Nations held out the promise of a world living in peace and harmony, and India, an equal partner with Britain, would be among the great nations...

A few weeks later, Bengal and Punjab provinces were bisected. Riots flared up across northern India, and there was a great exodus of people crossing the newly drawn frontiers of Pakistan and India. Homes were destroyed, thousands lost their lives.

The common-room radio and the occasional newspaper kept us abreast of events, but in our tunnel, Omar and I felt immune from all that was happening, worlds away from all the pillage, murder and revenge. And outside the tunnel, on the pine knoll below the school, there was fresh untrodden grass, sprinkled with clover and daisies, the only sounds the hammering of a woodpecker, the distant insistent call of the Himalayan barbet. Who could touch us there?

'And when all the wars are done,' I said, 'a butterfly will still be beautiful.'

'Did you read that somewhere?'

'No, it just came into my head.'

'Already you're a writer.'

'No, I want to play hockey for India or football for Arsenal. Only winning teams!'

'You can't win forever. Better to be a writer.'

When the monsoon rains arrived, the tunnel was flooded, the drain choked with rubble. We were allowed out to the cinema to see Lawrence Olivier's *Hamlet*, a film that did nothing to raise our spirits on a wet and gloomy afternoon—but it was our last picture that year, because communal riots suddenly broke out in Simla's Lower Bazaar, an area that was still much as Kipling had described it—'a man who knows his way there can defy all the police of India's summer capital'—and we were confined to school indefinitely.

One morning after chapel, the headmaster announced that the Muslim boys—those who had their homes in what was now Pakistan—would have to be evacuated, sent to their homes across the border with an armed convoy.

The tunnel no longer provided an escape for us. The bazaar was out of bounds. The flooded playing field was deserted. Omar and I sat on a damp wooden bench and talked about the future in vaguely hopeful terms; but we didn't solve any problems. Mountbatten and Nehru and Jinnah were doing all the solving.

It was soon time for Omar to leave—he along with some fifty

other boys from Lahore, Pindi and Peshawar. The rest of us—Hindus, Christians, Parsis—helped them load their luggage into the waiting trucks. A couple of boys broke down and wept. So did our departing school captain, a Pathan who had been known for his stoic and unemotional demeanour. Omar waved cheerfully to me and I waved back. We had vowed to meet again some day.

The convoy got through safely enough. There was only one casualty—the school cook, who had strayed into an off-limits area in the foothill town of Kalka and been set upon by a mob. He wasn't seen again.

Towards the end of the school year, just as we were all getting ready to leave for the school holidays, I received a letter from Omar. He told me something about his new school and how he missed my company and our games and our tunnel to freedom. I replied and gave him my home address, but I did not hear from him again. The land, though divided, was still a big one, and we were very small.

Some seventeen or eighteen years later I did get news of Omar, but in an entirely different context. India and Pakistan were at war and in a bombing raid over Ambala, not far from Simla, a Pakistani plane was shot down. Its crew died in the crash. One of them, I learnt later, was Omar.

Did he, I wonder, get a glimpse of the playing fields we knew so well as boys?

Perhaps memories of his schooldays flooded back as he flew over the foothills. Perhaps he remembered the tunnel through which we were able to make our little escape to freedom.

But there are no tunnels in the sky.

THE HARE IN THE MOON

A long time ago, when animals could talk, there lived in a forest four wise creatures—a hare, a jackal, an otter and a monkey.

They were good friends, and every evening they would sit together in a forest glade to discuss the events of the day, exchange advice, and make good resolutions. The hare was the noblest and wisest of the four. He believed in the superiority of men and women, and was always telling his friends tales of human goodness and wisdom.

One evening, when the moon rose in the sky—and in those days the moon's face was clear and unmarked—the hare looked up at it carefully and said: 'Tomorrow good men will observe a fast, for I can see that it will be the middle of the month. They will eat no food before sunset, and during the day they will give alms to any beggar or holy man who may meet them. Let us promise to do the same. In that way, we can come a little closer to human beings in dignity and wisdom.'

The others agreed, and then went their different ways.

Next day, the otter got up, stretched himself, and was preparing to get his breakfast when he remembered the vow he had taken with his friends.

If I keep my word, how hungry I shall be by evening! he thought. I'd better make sure that there's plenty to eat once the fast is over. He set off towards the river.

A fisherman had caught several large fish early that morning, and had buried them in the sand, planning to return for them later. The otter soon smelt them out.

'A supper all ready for me!' he said to himself. 'But since it's a holy day, I mustn't steal.' Instead he called out: 'Does anyone own this fish?'

There being no answer, the otter carried the fish off to his home, setting it aside for his evening meal. Then he locked his front door and slept all through the day, undisturbed by beggars or holy men asking for alms.

Both the monkey and the jackal felt much the same way when they got up that morning. They remembered their vows but thought it best to have something put by for the evening. The jackal found some stale meat in someone's backyard. *Ah, that should improve with age*, he thought, and took it home for his evening meal. And the monkey climbed a mango tree and picked a bunch of mangoes. Like the otter, they decided to sleep through the day.

The hare woke early. Shaking his long ears, he came out of his burrow and sniffed the dew-drenched grass.

When evening comes, I can have my fill of grass, he thought. *But if a beggar or holy man comes my way, what can I give him? I cannot offer him grass, and I have nothing else to give. I shall have to offer myself. Most men seem to relish the flesh of the hare. We're good to eat, I'm told.* And pleased with this solution to the problem, he scampered off.

Now, the God Sakka had been resting on a cloud not far away, and he had heard the hare speaking aloud.

'I will test him,' said the god. 'Surely no hare can be so noble and unselfish.'

Towards evening, God Sakka descended from his cloud, and assuming the form of an old priest, he sat down near the hare's burrow. When the animal came home from his romp, he said: 'Good evening, little hare. Can you give me something to eat? I have been fasting all day, and am so hungry that I cannot pray.'

The hare, remembering his vow, said: 'Is it true that men enjoy eating the flesh of the hare?'

'Quite true,' said the priest.

'In that case,' said the hare, 'since I have no other food to offer you, you can make a meal of me.'

'But I am a holy man, and this is a holy day, and I may not kill any living creature with my own hands.'

'Then collect some dry sticks and set them alight. I will leap into the flames myself, and when I am roasted you can eat me.'

God Sakka marvelled at these words, but he was still not quite convinced, so he caused a fire to spring up from the earth. The hare, without any hesitation, jumped into the flames.

'What's happening?' called the hare after a while. 'The fire surrounds me, but not a hair of my coat is singed. In fact, I'm feeling quite cold!'

As the hare spoke, the fire died down, and he found himself sitting on the cool sweet grass. Instead of the old priest, there stood before him the God Sakka in all his radiance.

'I am God Sakka, little hare, and having heard your vow, I wanted to test your sincerity. Such unselfishness of yours deserves immortality. It must be known throughout the world.'

God Sakka then stretched out his hand towards the mountain, and drew from it some of the essence which ran in its veins. This he threw towards the moon, which had just risen, and instantly the outline of the hare appeared on the moon's surface.

Then leaving the hare in a bed of sweet grass, he said: 'For ever and ever, little hare, you shall look down from the moon upon the world, to remind men of the old truth, "Give to others, and the gods will give to you."'

FROM SMALL BEGINNINGS

> *And the last puff of the day-wind brought from the unseen villages the scent of damp wood-smoke, hot cakes, dripping undergrowth, and rotting pine-cones. That is the true smell of the Himalayas, and if once it creeps into the blood of a man, that man will at the last, forgetting all else, return to the hills to die.*
>
> —Rudyard Kipling

On the first clear September day, towards the end of the rains, I visited the pine knoll, my place of peace and power. It was months since I'd last been there. Trips to the plains, a crisis in my affairs, involvements with other people and their troubles, and an entire monsoon had come between me and the grassy, pine-topped slope facing the Hill of Fairies (Pari Tibba to the locals). Now I tramped through late monsoon foliage—tall ferns, bushes festooned with flowering convolvulus—and crossed the stream by way of its little bridge of stones before climbing the steep hill to the pine slope.

When the trees saw me, they made as if to turn in my direction. A puff of wind came across the valley from the distant snows. A long-tailed blue magpie took alarm and flew noisily out of an oak tree. The cicadas were suddenly silent. But the trees remembered me. They bowed gently in the breeze and beckoned me nearer, welcoming me home. Three pines, a straggling oak and a wild cherry. I went among them and acknowledged their welcome with a touch of my hand against their trunks—the cherry's smooth and polished; the pine's patterned and whorled; the oak's rough, gnarled, full of experience. He'd been there the longest, and the wind had bent his upper branches and twisted a few, so that he looked shaggy and undistinguished. But like the philosopher who is careless about his dress and appearance, the oak has secrets, a hidden wisdom. He has learnt the art of survival!

While the oak and the pines are older than me and have been here many years, the cherry tree is exactly seven years old. I know, because I planted it.

One day I had this cherry seed in my hand, and on an impulse I thrust it into the soft earth, and then went away and forgot all about it. A few months later I found a tiny cherry tree in the long grass. I did not expect it to survive. But the following year it was two feet tall. And then some goats ate its leaves and a grass cutter's scythe injured the stem, and I was sure it would wither away. But it renewed itself, sprang up even faster, and within three years it was a healthy, growing tree, about five feet tall.

I left the hills for two years—forced by circumstances to make a living in Delhi—but this time I did not forget the cherry tree. I thought about it fairly often, sent telepathic messages of encouragement in its direction. And when, a couple of years ago, I returned in the autumn, my heart did a somersault when I found my tree sprinkled with pale pink blossom. (The Himalayan cherry flowers in November.) And later, when the fruit was ripe, the tree was visited by finches, tits, bulbuls and other small birds, all come to feast on the sour, red cherries.

Last summer I spent a night on the pine knoll, sleeping on the grass beneath the cherry tree. I lay awake for hours, listening to the chatter of the stream and the occasional *tonk-tonk* of nightjars, and watching through the branches overhead, the stars turning in the sky. And I felt the power of the sky and the earth, and the power of a small cherry seed...

And so when the rains are over, this is where I come, that I might feel the peace and power of this place.

This is where I will write my stories. I can see everything from here—my cottage across the valley; behind and above me, the town and the bazaar, straddling the ridge; to the left, the high mountains and the twisting road to the source of the great river; below me, the little stream and the path to the village; ahead, the Hill of Fairies and the fields beyond; the wide valley below, and another range of hills and then the distant plains. I can even see Prem Singh in the garden, putting the mattresses out in the sun.

From here he is just a speck on the far hill, but I know it is Prem by the way he stands. A man may have a hundred disguises, but in the end it is his posture that gives him away. Like my grandfather, who was a master of disguise and successfully roamed the bazaars as fruit vendor or basket maker. But we could always recognize him because of his pronounced slouch.

Prem Singh doesn't slouch, but he has this habit of looking up at the sky (regardless of whether it's cloudy or clear), and at the moment he's looking at the sky.

Eight years with Prem. He was just a sixteen-year-old boy when I first saw him, and now he has a wife and child.

I had been in the cottage for just over a year... He stood on the landing outside the kitchen door. A tall boy, dark, with good teeth and brown, deep-set eyes, dressed smartly in white drill—his only change of clothes. Looking for a job. I liked the look of him, but—

'I already have someone working for me,' I said.

'Yes, sir. He is my uncle.'

In the hills, everyone is a brother or an uncle.

'You don't want me to dismiss your uncle?'

'No, sir. But he says you can find a job for me.'

'I'll try. I'll make inquiries. Have you just come from your village?'

'Yes. Yesterday I walked ten miles to Pauri. There I got a bus.'

'Sit down. Your uncle will make some tea.'

He sat down on the steps, removed his white keds, wriggled his toes. His feet were both long and broad, large feet but not ugly. He was unusually clean for a hill boy. And taller than most.

'Do you smoke?' I asked.

'No, sir.'

'It is true,' said his uncle. 'He does not smoke. All my nephews smoke but this one. He is a little peculiar, he does not smoke—neither beedi nor hookah.'

'Do you drink?'

'It makes me vomit.'

'Do you take bhang?'

'No, sahib.'

'You have no vices. It's unnatural.'

'He is unnatural, sahib,' said his uncle.

'Does he chase girls?'

'They chase him, sahib.'

'So he left the village and came looking for a job.' I looked at him. He grinned, then looked away and began rubbing his feet.

'Your name is...?'

'Prem Singh.'

'All right, Prem, I will try to do something for you.'

I did not see him for a couple of weeks. I forgot about finding him a job. But when I met him again, on the road to the bazaar, he told me that he had got a temporary job in the Survey, looking after the surveyor's tents.

'Next week we will be going to Rajasthan,' he said.

'It will be very hot. Have you been in the desert before?'

'No, sir.'

'It is not like the hills. And it is far from home.'

'I know. But I have no choice in the matter. I have to collect some money in order to get married.'

In his region there was a bride price, usually of 2,000 rupees.

'Do you have to get married so soon?'

'I have only one brother and he is still very young. My mother is not well. She needs a daughter-in-law to help her in the fields and the house, and with the cows. We are a small family, so the work is greater.'

Every family has its few terraced fields, narrow and stony, usually perched on a hillside above a stream or river. They grow rice, barley, maize, potatoes—just enough to live on. Even if their produce is sufficient for marketing, the absence of roads makes it difficult to get the produce to the market towns. There is no money to be earned in the villages, and money is needed for clothes, soap, medicines, and for recovering the family jewellery from the moneylenders. So the young men leave their villages to find work, and to find work they must go to the plains. The lucky ones get into the army. Others enter domestic service or take jobs in garages, hotels, wayside tea shops, schools…

In Mussoorie the main attraction is the large number of schools which employ cooks and bearers. But the schools were full when Prem arrived. He'd been to the recruiting centre at Roorkee, hoping to get into the army; but they found a deformity in his right foot, the result of a bone broken when a landslip carried him away one dark monsoon night. He was lucky, he said, that it was only his foot and not his head that had been broken.

He came to the house to inform his uncle about the job and to say goodbye. I thought, another nice person I probably won't see again; another ship passing in the night, the friendly twinkle of its lights soon vanishing in the darkness. I said 'Come again', held his smile with mine so that I could remember him better, and returned to my study and my typewriter. The typewriter is the repository of a writer's loneliness. It stares unsympathetically back at him every day, doing its best to be discouraging. Maybe I'll go back to the old-fashioned quill pen and marble inkstand; then I can feel like a real writer—Balzac or Dickens—scratching away into the endless reaches of the night... Of course, the days and nights are seemingly shorter than they need to be! They must be, otherwise why do we hurry so much and achieve so little, by the standards of the past...

Prem goes, disappears into the vast faceless cities of the plains, and a year slips by, or rather I do, and then here he is again, thinner and darker and still smiling and still looking for a job. I should have known that hillmen don't disappear altogether. The spirit-haunted rocks don't let their people wander too far, lest they lose them forever.

I was able to get him a job in the school. The headmaster's wife needed a cook. I wasn't sure if Prem could cook very well but I sent him along and they said they'd give him a trial. Three days later the headmaster's wife met me on the road and started gushing all over me. She was the type who gushed.

'We're so grateful to you! Thank you for sending me that lovely boy. He's so polite. And he cooks very well. A little too hot for my husband, but otherwise delicious—just delicious! He's a real treasure—a lovely boy.' And she gave me an arch look—the famous look which she used to captivate all the good-looking young prefects who became prefects, it was said, only if she approved of them.

I wasn't sure that she didn't want something more than a cook, and I only hoped that Prem would give every satisfaction.

He looked cheerful enough when he came to see me on his off day.

'How are you getting on?' I asked.

'Lovely,' he said, using his mistress's favourite expression.

'What do you mean—lovely? Do they like your work?'

'The memsahib likes it. She strokes me on the cheek whenever she enters the kitchen. The sahib says nothing. He takes medicine after every meal.'

'Did he always take medicine—or only now that you're doing the cooking?'

'I am not sure. I think he has always been sick.'

He was sleeping in the headmaster's verandah and getting sixty rupees a month. A cook in Delhi got a hundred and sixty. And a cook in Paris or New York got ten times as much. I did not say as much to Prem. He might ask me to get him a job in New York. And that would be the last I saw of him! He, as a cook, might well get a job making curries off-Broadway; I, as a writer, wouldn't get to first base. And only my Uncle Ken knew the secret of how to make a living without actually doing any work. But then, of course, he had four sisters. And each of them was married to a fairly prosperous husband. So Uncle Ken divided his year among them. Three months with Aunt Ruby in Nainital. Three months with Aunt Susie in Kashmir. Three months with my mother (not quite so affluent) in Jamnagar. And three months in the Vet Hospital in Bareilly, where Aunt Mabel ran the hospital for her veterinary husband. In this way he never overstayed his welcome. A sister can look after a brother for just three months at a time and no more. Uncle K had it worked out to perfection.

But I had no sisters and I couldn't live forever on the royalties of a single novel. So I had to write others. So I came to the hills.

The hillmen go to the plains to make a living. I had to come to the hills to try and make mine.

'Prem,' I said, 'why don't you work for me?'

'And what about my uncle?'

'He seems ready to desert me any day. His grandfather is ill, he says, and he wants to go home.'

'His grandfather died last year.'

'That's what I mean—he's getting restless. And I don't mind

if he goes. These days he seems to be suffering from a form of sleeping sickness. I have to get up first and make his tea...'

Sitting here under the cherry tree, whose leaves are just beginning to turn yellow, I rest my chin on my knees and gaze across the valley to where Prem moves about in the garden. Looking back over the seven years he has been with me, I recall some of the nicest things about him. They come to me in no particular order—just pieces of cinema—coloured slides slipping across the screen of memory...

Prem rocking his infant son to sleep—crooning to him, passing his large hand gently over the child's curly head—Prem following me down to the police station when I was arrested (on a warrant from Bombay, charging me with writing an allegedly obscene short story!), and waiting outside until I reappeared, his smile, when I found him in Delhi, his large, irrepressible laughter, most in evidence when he was seeing an old Laurel and Hardy movie.

Of course, there were times when he could be infuriating, stubborn, deliberately pig-headed, sending me little notes of resignation—but I never found it difficult to overlook these little acts of self-indulgence. He had brought much love and laughter into my life, and what more could a lonely man ask for?

It was his stubborn streak that limited the length of his stay in the headmaster's household. Mr Good was tolerant enough. But Mrs Good was one of those women who, when they are pleased with you, go out of their way to help, pamper and flatter, but when displeased, become vindictive, going out of their way to harm or destroy. Mrs Good sought power—over her husband, her dog, her favourite pupils, her servant... She had absolute power over the husband and the dog, partial power over her slightly bewildered pupils, and none at all over Prem, who missed the subtleties of her designs upon his soul. He did not respond to her mothering, or to the way in which she tweaked him on the cheeks, brushed against him in the kitchen and made admiring remarks about his looks and physique. Memsahibs, he knew, were not for him. So he kept a stony face and went diligently about his duties. And she felt slighted, put in her place. Her liking turned to dislike. Instead of admiring remarks, she began making disparaging remarks about his looks, his clothes, his manners. She found fault with his cooking. No longer was it 'lovely'. She even accused him of taking away the dog's meat and giving it to a poor family living on the hillside—no more heinous crime could be imagined! Mr Good threatened him with dismissal. So Prem became stubborn. The following day he withheld the dog's food altogether, threw it down the khud where it was seized upon by innumerable strays, and went off to the pictures.

That was the end of his job. 'I'll have to go home now,' he told me. 'I won't get another job in this area. The mem will see to that.'

'Stay a few days,' I said.

'I have only enough money with which to get home.'

'Keep it for going home. You can stay with me for a few days, while you look around. Your uncle won't mind sharing his food with you.'

His uncle did mind. He did not like the idea of working for his nephew as well; it seemed to him no part of his duties. And he was apprehensive that Prem might get his job.

So Prem stayed no longer than a week.

Here on the knoll the grass is just beginning to turn October yellow. The first clouds approaching winter cover the sky. The trees are very still. The birds are silent. Only a cricket keeps singing on the oak tree. Perhaps there will be a storm before evening. A storm like the one in which Prem arrived at the cottage with his wife and child—but that's jumping too far ahead...

After he had returned to his village, it was several months before I saw him again. His uncle told me he had taken up a job in Delhi. There was an address. It did not seem complete, but I resolved that when I was next in Delhi I would try to see him.

The opportunity came in May, as the hot winds of summer blew across the plains. It was the time of year when people who can afford it, try to get away to the hills. I dislike New Delhi at the best of times, and I hate it in summer. People compete with each other in being bad-tempered and mean. But I had to go down—I don't remember why, but it must have seemed very necessary at the time—and I took the opportunity to try and see Prem.

Nothing went right for me. Of course the address was all wrong, and I wandered about in a remote, dusty, treeless colony called Vasant Vihar (Spring Garden) for over two hours, asking all the domestic servants I came across if they could put me in touch with Prem Singh of Village Koli, Pauri Garhwal. There were innumerable Prem Singhs, but apparently none who belonged to Village Koli. I returned to my hotel and took two days to recover from heatstroke before returning to Mussoorie, thanking God for mountains!

And then the uncle gave notice. He'd found a better-paid job in Dehradun and was anxious to be off. I didn't try to stop him.

For the next six months I lived in the cottage without any help. I did not find this difficult. I was used to living alone. It wasn't service that I needed but companionship. In the cottage it was very quiet. The ghosts of long-dead residents were sympathetic but unobtrusive. The song of the whistling thrush was beautiful, but I knew he was not singing for me. Up the valley came the sound of a flute, but I never saw the flute player. My affinity was with the little red fox who roamed the hillside below the cottage. I met him one night and wrote these lines:

As I walked home last night
I saw a lone fox dancing
In the cold moonlight.

I stood and watched—then
Took the low road, knowing
the night was his by right.
Sometimes, when words ring true,
I'm like a lone fox dancing
In the morning dew.

During the rains, watching the dripping trees and the mist climbing the valley, I wrote a great deal of poetry. Loneliness is of value to poets. But poetry didn't bring me much money, and funds were low. And then, just as I was wondering if I would have to give up my freedom and take a job again, a publisher bought the paperback rights of one of my children's stories, and I was free to live and write as I pleased—for another three months!

That was in November. To celebrate, I took a long walk through the Landour bazaar and up the Tehri road. It was a good day for walking; and it was dark by the time I returned to the outskirts of the town. Someone stood waiting for me on the road above the cottage. I hurried past him.

If I am not for myself,
Who will be for me?
And if I am not for others,
What am I?
And if not now, when?

I startled myself with the memory of these words of Hillel, the ancient Hebrew sage. I walked back to the shadows where the youth stood, and saw that it was Prem.

'Prem!' I said. 'Why are you sitting out here, in the cold? Why did you not go to the house?'

'I went, sir, but there was a lock on the door. I thought you had gone away.'

'And you were going to remain here, on the road?'

'Only for tonight. I would have gone down to Dehra in the morning.'

'Come, let's go home. I have been waiting for you. I looked for you in Delhi, but could not find the place where you were working.'

'I have left them now.'

'And your uncle has left me. So will you work for me now?'

'For as long as you wish.'

'For as long as the gods wish.'

We did not go straight home, but returned to the bazaar and took our meal in the Sindhi Sweet Shop—hot puris and strong sweet tea.

We walked home together in the bright moonlight. I felt sorry for the little fox dancing alone.

That was twenty years ago, and Prem and his wife and three children are still with me. But we live in a different house now, on another hill.

A LONG WALK FOR BINA

1

A leopard, lithe and sinewy, drank at the mountain stream, and then lay down on the grass to bask in the late February sunshine. Its tail twitched occasionally and the animal appeared to be sleeping. At the sound of distant voices it raised its head to listen, then stood up and leapt lightly over the boulders in the stream, disappearing among the trees on the opposite bank.

A minute or two later, three children came walking down the forest path. They were a girl and two boys, and they were singing in their local dialect an old song they had learnt from their grandparents.

> Five more miles to go!
> We climb through rain and snow.
> A river to cross...
> A mountain to pass...
> Now we've four more miles to go!

Their school satchels looked new, their clothes had been washed and pressed. Their loud and cheerful singing startled a Spotted Forktail. The bird left its favourite rock in the stream and flew down the dark ravine.

'Well, we have only three more miles to go,' said the bigger boy, Prakash, who had been this way hundreds of times. 'But first we have to cross the stream.'

He was a sturdy twelve-year-old with eyes like black currants and a mop of bushy hair that refused to settle down on his head. The girl and her small brother were taking this path for the first time.

'I'm feeling tired, Bina,' said the little boy.

Bina smiled at him, and Prakash said, 'Don't worry, Sonu, you'll get used to the walk. There's plenty of time.' He glanced at the old watch he'd been given by his grandfather. It needed constant winding. 'We can rest here for five or six minutes.'

They sat down on a smooth boulder and watched the clear water of the shallow stream tumbling downhill. Bina examined the old watch on Prakash's wrist. The glass was badly scratched and she could barely make out the figure on the dial. 'Are you sure it still gives the right time?' she asked.

'Well, it loses five minutes every day, so I put it ten minutes forward at night. That means by morning it's quite accurate! Even our teacher, Mr Mani, asks me for the time. If he doesn't ask, I tell him! The clock in our classroom keeps stopping.'

They removed their shoes and let the cold mountain water run over their feet. Bina was the same age as Prakash. She had pink cheeks, soft brown eyes and hair that was just beginning to lose its natural curls. Hers was a gentle face, but a determined little chin showed that she could be a strong person. Sonu, her younger brother, was ten. He was a thin boy who had been sickly as a child but was now beginning to fill out. Although he did not look very athletic, he could run like the wind.

■

Bina had been going to school in her own village of Koli, on the other side of the mountain. But it had been a Primary School, finishing at Class 5. Now, in order to study in Class 6, she would have to walk several miles every day to Nauti, where there was a High School going up to Class 8. It had been decided that Sonu would also shift to the new school, to give Bina company. Prakash, their neighbour in Koli, was already a pupil at the Nauti school. His mischievous nature, which sometimes got him into trouble, had resulted in his having to repeat a year.

But this didn't seem to bother him. 'What's the hurry?' he had told his indignant parents. 'You're not sending me to a foreign land when I finish school. And our cows aren't running away, are they?'

'You would prefer to look after the cows, wouldn't you?' asked Bina, as they got up to continue their walk.

'Oh, school's all right. Wait till you see old Mr Mani. He always gets our names mixed up, as well as the subjects he's supposed to be teaching. At our last lesson, instead of maths, he gave us a geography lesson!'

'More fun than maths,' said Bina.

'Yes, but there's a new teacher this year. She's very young they say, just out of college. I wonder what she'll be like.'

Bina walked faster and Sonu had some trouble keeping up with them. She was excited about the new school and the prospect of different surroundings. She had seldom been outside her own village, with its small school and single ration shop. The day's routine never varied—helping her mother in the fields or with household tasks like fetching water from the spring or cutting grass and fodder for the cattle. Her father, who was a soldier, was away for nine months in the year and Sonu was still too small for the heavier tasks.

As they neared Nauti village, they were joined by other children coming from different directions. Even where there were no major roads, the mountains were full of little lanes and shortcuts. Like a game of snakes and ladders, these narrow paths zigzagged around the hills and villages, cutting through fields and crossing narrow ravines until they came together to form a fairly busy road along which mules, cattle and goats joined the throng.

Nauti was a fairly large village, and from here a broader but dustier road started for Tehri. There was a small bus, several trucks and (for part of the way) a road roller. The road hadn't been completed because the heavy diesel roller couldn't take the steep climb to Nauti. It stood on the roadside halfway up the road from Tehri.

Prakash knew almost everyone in the area, and exchanged greetings and gossip with other children as well as with muleteers, bus drivers, milkmen and labourers working on the road. He loved telling everyone the time, even if they weren't interested.

'It's nine o'clock,' he would announce, glancing at his wrist. 'Isn't your bus leaving today?'

'Off with you!' the bus driver would respond, 'I'll leave when I'm ready.'

As the children approached Nauti, the small flat school buildings came into view on the outskirts of the village, fringed by a line of long-leaved pines. A small crowd had assembled on the one playing field. Something unusual seemed to have happened. Prakash ran forward to see what it was all about. Bina and Sonu stood aside, waiting in a patch of sunlight near the boundary wall.

Prakash soon came running back to them. He was bubbling over with excitement.

'It's Mr Mani!' he gasped. 'He's disappeared! People are saying a leopard must have carried him off!'

2

Mr Mani wasn't really old. He was about fifty-five and was expected to retire soon. But for the children, most adults over forty seemed ancient! And Mr Mani had always been a bit absentminded, even as a young man.

He had gone out for his early morning walk, saying he'd be back by eight o'clock, in time to have his breakfast and be ready for class. He wasn't married, but his sister and her husband stayed with him. When it was past nine o'clock, his sister presumed he'd stopped at a neighbour's house for breakfast (he loved tucking into other people's breakfast) and that he had gone on to school from there. But when the school bell rang at ten o'clock, and everyone but Mr Mani was present, questions were asked and guesses were made.

No one had seen him return from his walk and enquiries made in the village showed that he had not stopped at anyone's house. For Mr Mani to disappear was puzzling; for him to disappear without his breakfast was extraordinary.

Then a milkman returning from the next village said he had seen a leopard sitting on a rock on the outskirts of the pine forest. There had been talk of a cattle-killer in the valley, of leopards and other animals being displaced by the constructions of a dam. But as yet no one had heard of a leopard attacking a man. Could Mr Mani have been its first victim? Someone found a strip of red cloth entangled in a blackberry bush and went running through the village showing it to everyone. Mr Mani had been known to wear red pyjamas. Surely he had been seized and eaten! But where were his remains? And why had he been in his pyjamas?

Meanwhile, Bina and Sonu and the rest of the children had followed their teachers into the school playground. Feeling a little lost, Bina looked around for Prakash. She found herself facing a dark slender young woman wearing spectacles, who must have been in her early twenties—just a little too old to be another student. She had a kind, expressive face and she seemed a little concerned by all that had been happening.

Bina noticed that she had lovely hands; it was obvious that the new teacher hadn't milked cows or worked in the fields!

'You must be new here,' said the teacher, smiling at Bina. 'And is this your little brother?'

'Yes, we've come from Koli village. We were at school there.'

'It's a long walk from Koli. You didn't see any leopards, did you? Well, I'm new too. Are you in the sixth class?'

'Sonu is in the third. I'm in the sixth.'

'Then I'm your new teacher. My name is Tania Ramola. Come along, let's see if we can settle down in our classroom.'

Mr Mani turned up at twelve o'clock, wondering what all the fuss was about. No, he snapped, he had not been attacked by a leopard; and yes, he had lost his pyjamas and would someone kindly return them to him?

'How did you lose your pyjamas, sir?' asked Prakash.

'They were blown off the washing line!' snapped Mr Mani.

After much questioning, Mr Mani admitted that he had gone further than he had intended, and that he had lost his way coming back. He had been a bit upset because the new teacher, a slip of a girl, had been given charge of the sixth, while he was still with the fifth, along with that troublesome boy Prakash, who kept on reminding him of the time! The headmaster had explained that as Mr Mani was due to retire at the end of the year, the school did not wish to burden him with a senior class. But Mr Mani looked upon the whole thing as a plot to get rid of him. He glowered at Miss Ramola whenever he passed her. And when she smiled back at him, he looked the other way!

Mr Mani had been getting even more absentminded of late—putting on his shoes without his socks, wearing his homespun waistcoat inside out, mixing up people's names and, of course, eating other people's lunches and dinners. His sister had made a mutton broth for the postmaster, who was down with 'flu' and had asked Mr Mani to take it over in a thermos. When the postmaster opened the thermos, he found only a few drops of broth at the bottom—Mr Mani had drunk the rest somewhere along the way.

When sometimes Mr Mani spoke of his coming retirement, it was to describe his plans for the small field he owned just behind the house. Right now, it was full of potatoes, which did not require much looking after; but he had plans for growing dahlias, roses, French beans, and other fruits and flowers.

The next time he visited Tehri, he promised himself, he would buy some dahlia bulbs and rose cuttings. The monsoon season would be a good time to put them down. And meanwhile, his potatoes were still flourishing.

3

Bina enjoyed her first day at the new school. She felt at ease with Miss Ramola, as did most of the boys and girls in her class. Tania Ramola had been to distant towns such as Delhi and Lucknow—places they had only heard about—and it was said that she had a brother who was a pilot and flew planes all over the world. Perhaps he'd fly over Nauti some day!

Most of the children had of course seen planes flying overhead, but none of them had seen a ship, and only a few had been in a train. Tehri mountain was far from the railway and hundreds of miles from the sea. But they all knew about the big dam that was being built at Tehri, just forty miles away.

Bina, Sonu and Prakash had company for part of the way home, but gradually the other children went off in different directions. Once they had crossed the stream, they were on their own again.

It was a steep climb all the way back to their village. Prakash had a supply of peanuts which he shared with Bina and Sonu, and at a small spring they quenched their thirst.

When they were less than a mile from home, they met a

postman who had finished his round of the villages in the area and was now returning to Nauti.

'Don't waste time along the way,' he told them. 'Try to get home before dark.'

'What's the hurry?' asked Prakash, glancing at his watch. 'It's only five o'clock.'

'There's a leopard around. I saw it this morning, not far from the stream. No one is sure how it got here. So don't take any chances. Get home early.'

'So there really is a leopard,' said Sonu.

They took his advice and walked faster, and Sonu forgot to complain about his aching feet.

They were home well before sunset.

There was a smell of cooking in the air and they were hungry.

'Cabbage and roti,' said Prakash gloomily. 'But I could eat anything today.' He stopped outside his small slate-roofed house, and Bina and Sonu waved goodbye and carried on across a couple of ploughed fields until they reached their small stone house.

'Stuffed tomatoes,' said Sonu, sniffing just outside the front door.

'And lemon pickle,' said Bina, who had helped cut, sun and salt the lemons a month previously.

Their mother was lighting the kitchen stove. They greeted her with great hugs and demands for an immediate dinner. She was a good cook who could make even the simplest of dishes taste delicious. Her favourite saying was, 'Home-made bread is better than roast meat abroad,' and Bina and Sonu had to agree.

Electricity had yet to reach their village, and they took their meal by the light of a kerosene lamp. After the meal, Sonu settled down to do a little homework, while Bina stepped outside to look at the stars.

Across the fields, someone was playing a flute. 'It must be

Prakash,' thought Bina. 'He always breaks off on the high notes.' But the flute music was simple and appealing, and she began singing softly to herself in the dark.

4

Mr Mani was having trouble with the porcupines. They had been getting into his garden at night and digging up and eating his potatoes. From his bedroom window—left open, now that the mild April weather had arrived—he could listen to them enjoying the vegetables he had worked hard to grow. Scrunch, scrunch! *Katar, katar*, as their sharp teeth sliced through the largest and juiciest of potatoes. For Mr Mani it was as though they were biting through his own flesh. And the sound of them digging industriously as they rooted up those healthy, leafy plants made him tremble with rage and indignation. The unfairness of it all!

Yes, Mr Mani hated porcupines. He prayed for their destruction, their removal from the face of the earth. But, as his friends were quick to point out, 'The creator made porcupines too,' and in any case you could never see the creatures or catch them, they were completely nocturnal.

Mr Mani got out of bed every night, torch in one hand, a stout stick in the other but, as soon as he stepped into the garden, the crunching and digging stopped and he was greeted by the most infuriating of silences. He would grope around in the dark, swinging wildly with the stick, but not a single porcupine was to be seen or heard. As soon as he was back in bed, the sounds would start all over again—scrunch, scrunch, *katar, katar*...

Mr Mani came to his class tired and dishevelled, with rings beneath his eyes and a permanent frown on his face. It took some time for his pupils to discover the reason for his misery, but when they did, they felt sorry for their teacher and took to discussing ways and means of saving his potatoes from the porcupines.

It was Prakash who came up with the idea of a moat or water ditch. 'Porcupines don't like water,' he said knowledgeably.

'How do you know?' asked one of his friends.

'Throw water on one and see how it runs! They don't like getting their quills wet.'

There was no one who could disprove Prakash's theory, and the class fell in with the idea of building a moat, especially as it meant getting most of the day off.

'Anything to make Mr Mani happy,' said the Headmaster, and the rest of the school watched with envy as the pupils of Class 5, armed with spades and shovels collected from all parts of the village, took up their positions around Mr Mani's potato field and began digging a ditch.

By evening the moat was ready, but it was still dry and the porcupines got in again that night and had a great feast.

'At this rate,' said Mr Mani gloomily, 'there won't be any potatoes left to save.'

But the next day, Prakash and the other boys and girls managed to divert the water from a stream that flowed past the village. They had the satisfaction of watching it flow gently into the ditch. Everyone went home in a good mood. By nightfall, the ditch had overflowed, the potato field was flooded, and Mr Mani found himself trapped inside his house. But Prakash and his friends had won the day. The porcupines stayed away that night!

▪

A month had passed, and wild violets, daisies and buttercups now sprinkled the hill slopes and, on her way to school, Bina gathered enough to make a little posy. The bunch of flowers fitted easily into an old ink well. Miss Ramola was delighted to find this little display in the middle of her desk.

'Who put these here?' she asked in surprise.

Bina kept quiet, and the rest of the class smiled secretively. After that, they took turns bringing flowers for the classroom.

On her long walks to school and home again, Bina became aware that April was the month of new leaves. The oak leaves were bright green above and silver beneath, and when they rippled in the breeze they were clouds of silvery green. The path was strewn with old leaves, dry and crackly. Sonu loved kicking them around.

Clouds of white butterflies floated across the stream. Sonu was chasing a butterfly when he stumbled over something dark and repulsive. He went sprawling on the grass. When he got to his feet, he looked down at the remains of a small animal.

'Bina! Prakash! Come quickly!' he shouted.

It was part of a sheep, killed some days earlier by a much larger animal.

'Only a leopard could have done this,' said Prakash.

'Let's get away, then,' said Sonu. 'It might still be around!'

'No, there's nothing left to eat. The leopard will be hunting elsewhere by now. Perhaps it's moved on to the next valley.'

'Still, I'm frightened,' said Sonu. 'There may be more leopards!'

Bina took him by the hand. 'Leopards don't attack humans!' she said.

'They will, if they get a taste for people!' insisted Prakash.

'Well, this one hasn't attacked any people as yet,' said Bina, although she couldn't be sure. Hadn't there been rumours of a leopard attacking some workers near the dam? But she did not want Sonu to feel afraid, so she did not mention the story. All she said was, 'It has probably come here because of all the activity near the dam.'

All the same, they hurried home. And for a few days, whenever they reached the stream, they crossed over very quickly, unwilling to linger too long at that lovely spot.

5

A few days later, a school party was on its way to Tehri to see the new dam that was being built.

Miss Ramola had arranged to take her class, and Mr Mani, not wishing to be left out, insisted on taking his class as well. That meant there were about fifty boys and girls taking part in the outing. The little bus could only take thirty. A friendly truck driver agreed to take some children if they were prepared to sit on sacks of potatoes. And Prakash persuaded the owner of the diesel-roller to turn it round and head it back to Tehri—with him and a couple of friends up on the driving seat.

Prakash's small group set off at sunrise, as they had to walk some distance in order to reach the stranded road roller. The bus left at 9 a.m. with Miss Ramola and her class, and Mr Mani and some of his pupils. The truck was to follow later.

It was Bina's first visit to a large town, and her first bus ride.

The sharp curves along the winding, downhill road made several children feel sick. The bus driver seemed to be in a tearing hurry. He took them along at a rolling, rollicking speed, which made Bina feel quite giddy. She rested her head on her arms and refused to look out of the window. Hairpin bends and cliff edges, pine forests and snowcapped peaks, all swept past her, but she felt too ill to want to look at anything. It was just as well—those sudden drops, hundreds of feet to the valley below, were quite frightening. Bina began to wish that she hadn't come—or that she had joined Prakash on the road roller instead!

Miss Ramola and Mr Mani didn't seem to notice the lurching and groaning of the old bus. They had made this journey many times. They were busy arguing about the advantages and disadvantages of large dams—an argument that was to continue on and off for much of the day.

Meanwhile, Prakash and his friends had reached the roller. The driver hadn't turned up, but they managed to reverse it and get it going in the direction of Tehri. They were soon overtaken by both bus and truck but kept moving along at a steady chug. Prakash spotted Bina at the window of the bus and waved cheerfully. She responded feebly.

Bina felt better when the road levelled out near Tehri. As they crossed an old bridge over the wide river, they were startled by a loud bang which made the bus shudder. A cloud of dust rose above the town.

'They're blasting the mountain,' said Miss Ramola.

'End of a mountain,' said Mr Mani, mournfully.

While they were drinking cups of tea at the bus stop, waiting for the potato truck and the road roller, Miss Ramola and Mr Mani continued their argument about the dam. Miss Ramola maintained that it would bring electric power and water for irrigation to large areas of the country, including the surrounding area. Mr Mani declared that it was a menace, as it was situated in an earthquake zone. There would be a terrible disaster if the dam burst! Bina found it all very confusing. And what about the animals in the area, she wondered, what would happen to them?

The argument was becoming quite heated when the potato truck arrived. There was no sign of the road roller, so it was decided that Mr Mani should wait for Prakash and his friends while Miss Ramola's group went ahead.

▪

Some eight or nine miles before Tehri, the road roller had broken down, and Prakash and his friends were forced to walk. They had not gone far, however, when a mule train came along—five or six mules that had been delivering sacks of grain in Nauti.

A boy rode on the first mule, but the others had no loads.

'Can you give us a ride to Tehri?' called Prakash.

'Make yourselves comfortable,' said the boy.

There were no saddles, only gunny sacks strapped on to the mules with rope. They had a rough but jolly ride down to the Tehri bus stop. None of them had ever ridden mules; but they had saved at least an hour on the road.

Looking around the bus stop for the rest of the party, they could find no one from their school. And Mr Mani, who should have been waiting for them, had vanished.

6

Tania Ramola and her group had taken the steep road to the hill above Tehri. Half an hour's climbing brought them to a little plateau which overlooked the town, the river and the dam site.

The earthworks for the dam were only just coming up, but a wide tunnel had been bored through the mountain to divert the river into another channel. Down below, the old town was still spread out across the valley and from a distance it looked quite charming and picturesque.

'Will the whole town be swallowed up by the waters of the dam?' asked Bina.

'Yes, all of it,' said Miss Ramola. 'The clock tower and the old palace. The long bazaar, and the temples, the schools and the jail, and hundreds of houses, for many miles up the valley. All those people will have to go—thousands of them! Of course they'll be resettled elsewhere.'

'But the town's been here for hundreds of years,' said Bina. 'They were quite happy without the dam, weren't they?'

'I suppose they were. But the dam isn't just for them—it's for the millions who live further downstream, across the plains.'

'And it doesn't matter what happens to this place?'

'The local people will be given new homes, somewhere else.' Miss Ramola found herself on the defensive and decided to change the subject. 'Everyone must be hungry. It's time we had our lunch.'

Bina kept quiet. She didn't think the local people would want to go away. And it was a good thing, she mused, that there was only a small stream and not a big river running past her village. To be uprooted like this—a town and hundreds of villages—and put down somewhere on the hot, dusty plains—seemed to her unbearable.

'Well, I'm glad I don't live in Tehri,' she said.

She did not know it, but all the animals and most of the birds had already left the area. The leopard had been among them.

▪

They walked through the colourful, crowded bazaar, where fruit sellers did business beside silversmiths, and pavement vendors sold everything from umbrellas to glass bangles. Sparrows attacked sacks of grain, monkeys made off with bananas, and stray cows and dogs rummaged in refuse bins, but nobody took any notice. Music blared from radios. Buses blew their horns. Sonu bought a whistle to add to the general din, but Miss Ramola told him to put it away. Bina had kept five rupees aside, and now she used it to buy a cotton headscarf for her mother.

As they were about to enter a small restaurant for a meal, they were joined by Prakash and his companions; but of Mr Mani there was still no sign.

'He must have met one of his relatives,' said Prakash. 'He has relatives everywhere.'

After a simple meal of rice and lentils, they walked the length of the bazaar without seeing Mr Mani. At last, when they were about to give up the search, they saw him emerge from a by-lane, a large sack slung over his shoulder.

'Sir, where have you been?' asked Prakash. 'We have been looking for you everywhere.'

On Mr Mani's face was a look of triumph.

'Help me with this bag,' he said breathlessly.

'You've bought more potatoes, sir,' said Prakash.

'Not potatoes, boy. Dahlia bulbs!'

7

It was dark by the time they were all back in Nauti. Mr Mani had refused to be separated from his sack of dahlia bulbs, and had been forced to sit in the back of the truck with Prakash and most of the boys.

Bina did not feel so ill on the return journey. Going uphill was definitely better than going downhill! But by the time the bus reached Nauti it was too late for most of the children to walk back to the more distant villages. The boys were put up in different homes, while the girls were given beds in the school verandah.

The night was warm and still. Large moths fluttered around the single bulb that lit the verandah. Counting moths, Sonu soon fell asleep. But Bina stayed awake for some time, listening to the sounds of the night. A nightjar went *tonk-tonk* in the bushes, and somewhere in the forest an owl hooted softly. The sharp call of a barking deer travelled up the valley, from the direction of the stream. Jackals kept howling. It seemed that there were more of them than ever before.

Bina was not the only one to hear the barking deer. The leopard, stretched full length on a rocky ledge, heard it too. The leopard raised its head and then got up slowly. The deer was its natural prey. But there weren't many left, and that was why the leopard, robbed of its forest by the dam, had taken to attacking dogs and cattle near the villages.

As the cry of the barking deer sounded nearer, the leopard left its lookout point and moved swiftly through the shadows towards the stream.

8

In early June, the hills were dry and dusty, and forest fires broke out, destroying shrubs and trees, killing birds and small animals. The resin in the pines made these trees burn more fiercely, and the wind would take sparks from the trees and carry them into the dry grass and leaves, so that new fires would spring up before the old ones had died out. Fortunately, Bina's village was not in the pine belt; the fires did not reach it. But Nauti was surrounded by a fire that raged for three days, and the children had to stay away from school.

And then, towards the end of June, the monsoon rains arrived and there was an end to forest fires. The monsoon lasts three months and the lower Himalayas would be drenched in rain, mist and cloud for the next three months.

The first rain arrived while Bina, Prakash and Sonu were returning home from school. Those first few drops on the dusty path made them cry out with excitement. Then the rain grew heavier and a wonderful aroma rose from the earth.

'The best smell in the world!' exclaimed Bina.

Everything suddenly came to life. The grass, the crops, the trees, the birds. Even the leaves of the trees glistened and looked new.

That first wet weekend, Bina and Sonu helped their mother plant beans, maize and cucumbers. Sometimes, when the rain was very heavy, they had to run indoors. Otherwise they worked in the rain, the soft mud clinging to their bare legs.

Prakash now owned a dog, a black dog with one ear up and one ear down. The dog ran around getting in everyone's way, barking at cows, goats, hens and humans, without frightening any of them. Prakash said it was a very clever dog, but no one else seemed to think so. Prakash also said it would protect the village from the leopard, but others said the dog would be the first to be taken—he'd run straight into the jaws of Mr Spots!

In Nauti, Tania Ramola was trying to find a dry spot in the quarters she'd been given. It was an old building and the roof was leaking in several places. Mugs and buckets were scattered about the floor in order to catch the drips.

Mr Mani had dug up all his potatoes and presented them to the friends and neighbours who had given him lunches and dinners. He was having the time of his life, planting dahlia bulbs all over his garden.

'I'll have a field of many-coloured dahlias!' he announced. 'Just wait till the end of August!'

'Watch out for those porcupines,' warned his sister. 'They eat dahlia bulbs too!'

Mr Mani made an inspection tour of his moat, no longer in flood, and found everything in good order. Prakash had done his job well.

■

Now, when the children crossed the stream, they found that the water level had risen by about a foot. Small cascades had turned into waterfalls. Ferns had sprung up on the banks. Frogs chanted.

Prakash and his dog dashed across the stream. Bina and Sonu followed more cautiously. The current was much stronger now and the water was almost up to their knees. Once they had crossed the stream, they hurried along the path, anxious not to be caught in a sudden downpour.

By the time they reached school, each of them had two or three leeches clinging to their legs. They had to use salt to remove them. The leeches were the most troublesome part of the rainy season. Even the leopard did not like them. It could not lie in the long grass without getting leeches on its paws and face.

One day, when Bina, Prakash and Sonu were about to cross the stream, they heard a low rumble, which grew louder every second. Looking up at the opposite hill, they saw several trees shudder, tilt outwards and begin to fall. Earth and rocks bulged out from the mountain, then came crashing down into the ravine.

'Landslide!' shouted Sonu.

'It's carried away the path,' said Bina. 'Don't go any further.'

There was a tremendous roar as more rocks, trees and bushes fell away and crashed down the hillside.

Prakash's dog, who had gone ahead, came running back, tail between his legs.

They remained rooted to the spot until the rocks had stopped falling and the dust had settled. Birds circled the area, calling wildly. A frightened barking deer ran past them.

'We can't go to school now,' said Prakash. 'There's no way around.'

They turned and trudged home through the gathering mist.

In Koli, Prakash's parents had heard the roar of the landslide. They were setting out in search of the children when they saw them emerge from the mist, waving cheerfully.

9

They had to miss school for another three days, and Bina was afraid they might not be able to take their final exams. Although Prakash was not really troubled at the thought of missing exams, he did not like feeling helpless just because their path had been swept away. So he explored the hillside until he found a goat-track going around the mountain. It joined up with another path near Nauti. This made their walk longer by a mile, but Bina did not mind. It was much cooler now that the rains were in full swing.

The only trouble with the new route was that it passed close to the leopard's lair. The animal had made this area its own since being forced to leave the dam area.

One day Prakash's dog ran ahead of them, barking furiously. Then he ran back, whimpering.

'He's always running away from something,' observed Sonu. But a minute later he understood the reason for the dog's fear.

They rounded a bend and Sonu saw the leopard standing in their way. They were struck dumb—too terrified to run. It was a strong, sinewy creature. A low growl rose from its throat. It seemed ready to spring.

They stood perfectly still, afraid to move or say a word. And the leopard must have been equally surprised. It stared at them for a few seconds, then bounded across the path and into the oak forest.

Sonu was shaking. Bina could hear her heart hammering. Prakash could only stammer: 'Did you see the way he sprang? Wasn't he beautiful?'

He forgot to look at his watch for the rest of the day.

A few days later, Sonu stopped and pointed to a large outcrop of rock on the next hill.

The leopard stood far above them, outlined against the sky. It looked strong, majestic. Standing beside it were two young cubs.

'Look at those little ones!' exclaimed Sonu.

'So it's a female, not a male,' said Prakash.

'That's why she was killing so often,' said Bina. 'She had to feed her cubs too.'

They remained still for several minutes, gazing up at the leopard and her cubs. The leopard family took no notice of them.

'She knows we are here,' said Prakash, 'but she doesn't care. She knows we won't harm them.'

'We are cubs too!' said Sonu.

'Yes,' said Bina. 'And there's still plenty of space for all of us. Even when the dam is ready there will still be room for leopards and humans.'

10

The school exams were over. The rains were nearly over too. The landslide had been cleared, and Bina, Prakash and Sonu were once again crossing the stream.

There was a chill in the air, for it was the end of September.

Prakash had learnt to play the flute quite well, and he played on the way to school and then again on the way home. As a result he did not look at his watch so often.

One morning, they found a small crowd in front of Mr Mani's house.

'What could have happened?' wondered Bina. 'I hope he hasn't got lost again.'

'Maybe he's sick,' said Sonu.

'Maybe it's the porcupines,' said Prakash.

But it was none of these things.

Mr Mani's first dahlia was in bloom, and half the village had turned up to look at it! It was a huge red double dahlia, so heavy that it had to be supported with sticks. No one had ever seen such a magnificent flower!

Mr Mani was a happy man. And his mood only improved over the coming week, as more and more dahlias flowered—crimson, yellow, purple, mauve, white—button dahlias, pom-pom dahlias, spotted dahlias, striped dahlias... Mr Mani had them all! A dahlia even turned up on Tania Ramola's desk—he got along quite well with her now—and another brightened up the Headmaster's study.

A week later, on their way home—it was almost the last day of the school term—Bina, Prakash and Sonu talked about what they might do when they grew up.

'I think I'll become a teacher,' said Bina. 'I'll teach children about animals and birds, and trees and flowers.'

'Better than maths!' said Prakash.

'I'll be a pilot,' said Sonu. 'I want to fly a plane like Miss Ramola's brother.'

'And what about you, Prakash?' asked Bina.

Prakash just smiled and said, 'Maybe I'll be a flute player,' and he put the flute to his lips and played a sweet melody.

'Well, the world needs flute players too,' said Bina, as they fell into step beside him.

The leopard had been stalking a barking deer. She paused when she heard the flute and the voices of the children. Her own young ones were growing quickly, but the girl and the two boys did not look much older.

They had started singing their favourite song again.

'Five more miles to go!
We climb through rain and snow,
A river to cross...
A mountain to pass...
Now we've four more miles to go!'

The leopard waited until they had passed, before returning to the trail of the barking deer.

THE FUNERAL

'I don't think he should go,' said Aunt M.

'He's too small,' concurred Aunt B. 'He'll get upset and probably throw a tantrum. And you know Padre Lal doesn't like having children at funerals.'

The boy said nothing. He sat in the darkest corner of the darkened room, his face revealing nothing of what he thought and felt. His father's coffin lay in the next room, the lid fastened forever over the tired, wistful countenance of the man who had meant so much to the boy. Nobody else had mattered—neither uncles nor aunts nor fond grandparents. Least of all the mother who was hundreds of miles away with another husband. He hadn't seen her since he was four—that was just over five years ago—and he did not remember her very well.

The house was full of people—friends, relatives, neighbours. Some had tried to fuss over him but had been discouraged by his silence, the absence of tears. The more understanding of them had kept their distance.

Scattered words of condolence passed back and forth like dragonflies on the wind. 'Such a tragedy!' … 'Only forty' … 'No one realized how serious it was' … 'Devoted to the child'…

It seemed to the boy that everyone who mattered in the hill station was present. And for the first time they had the run of the house for his father had not been a sociable man. Books, music, flowers and his stamp collection had been his main preoccupations, apart from the boy.

A small hearse, drawn by a hill pony, was led in at the gate and several able-bodied men lifted the coffin and manoeuvred it into the carriage. The crowd drifted away. The cemetery was about a mile down the road and those who did not have cars would have to walk the distance.

The boy stared through a window at the small procession passing through the gate. He'd been forgotten for the moment—left in care of the servants, who were the only ones to stay behind. Outside, it was misty. The mist had crept up the valley and settled like a damp towel on the face of the mountain. Everyone was wet although it hadn't rained.

The boy waited until everyone had gone and then he left the room and went out on the verandah. The gardener, who had been sitting in a bed of nasturtiums, looked up and asked the boy if he needed anything. But the boy shook his head and retreated indoors. The gardener, looking aggrieved because of the damage done to the flower beds by the mourners, shambled off to his quarters. The sahib's death meant that he would be out of a job very soon. The house would pass into other hands. The boy would go to an orphanage. There weren't many people who kept gardeners these days. In the kitchen, the cook was busy preparing the only big meal ever served in the house. All those relatives, and the padre too, would come back famished, ready for a sombre but nevertheless substantial meal. He, too, would be out of a job soon; but cooks were always in demand.

The boy slipped out of the house by a back door and made his way into the lane through a gap in a thicket of dog roses. When he reached the main road, he could see the mourners wending their way round the hill to the cemetery. He followed at a distance.

It was the same road he had often taken with his father during their evening walks. The boy knew the name of almost every plant and wildflower that grew on the hillside. These, and various birds and insects, had been described and pointed out to him by his father.

Looking northwards, he could see the higher ranges of the

Himalayas and the eternal snows. The graves in the cemetery were so laid out that if their incumbents did happen to rise one day, the first thing they would see would be the glint of the sun on those snow-covered peaks. Possibly the site had been chosen for the view. But to the boy it did not seem as if anyone would be able to thrust aside those massive tombstones and rise from their graves to enjoy the view. Their rest seemed as eternal as the snows. It would take an earthquake to burst those stones asunder and thrust the coffins up from the earth. The boy wondered why people hadn't made it easier for the dead to rise. They were so securely entombed that it appeared as though no one really wanted them to get out.

'God has need of your father…' With those words a well-meaning missionary had tried to console him.

And had God, in the same way, laid claim to the thousands of men, women and children who had been put to rest here in these neat and serried rows? What could he have wanted them for? Of what use are we to God when we are dead, wondered the boy.

The cemetery gate stood open but the boy leant against the old stone wall and stared down at the mourners as they shuffled about with the unease of a batsman about to face a very fast bowler. Only this bowler was invisible and would come up stealthily and from behind.

Padre Lal's voice droned on through the funeral service and then the coffin was lowered—down, deep down. The boy was surprised at how far down it seemed to go! Was that other, better world down in the depths of the earth? How could anyone, even a Samson, push his way back to the surface again? Superman did it in comics, but his father was a gentle soul who wouldn't fight too hard against the earth and the grass and the roots of tiny trees. Or perhaps he'd grow into a tree and escape that way! 'If ever I'm put away like this,' thought the boy, 'I'll get into the root of a plant and then I'll become a flower and then maybe a bird will come and carry my seed away… I'll get out somehow!'

A few more words from the padre and then some of those present threw handfuls of earth over the coffin before moving away.

Slowly, in twos and threes, the mourners departed. The mist swallowed them up. They did not see the boy behind the wall. They were getting hungry.

He stood there until they had all gone. Then he noticed that the gardeners or caretakers were filling in the grave. He did not know whether to go forward or not. He was a little afraid. And it was too late now. The grave was almost covered.

He turned and walked away from the cemetery. The road stretched ahead of him, empty, swathed in mist. He was alone. What had his father said to him once? 'The strongest man in the world is he who stands alone.'

Well, he was alone, but at the moment he did not feel very strong.

For a moment, he thought his father was beside him, that they were together on one of their long walks. Instinctively he put out his hand, expecting his father's warm, comforting touch. But there was nothing there, nothing, no one…

He clenched his fists and pushed them deep down into his pockets. He lowered his head so that no one would see his tears. There were people in the mist, but he did not want to go near them for they had put his father away.

'He'll find a way out,' the boy said fiercely to himself. 'He'll get out somehow!'

THE EYES HAVE IT

I had the train compartment to myself up to Rohana, then a girl got in. The couple who saw her off was probably her parents. They seemed very anxious about her comfort and the woman gave the girl detailed instructions as to where to keep her things, when not to lean out of windows and how to avoid speaking to strangers.

They called their goodbyes and the train pulled out of the station. As I was totally blind at the time, my eyes sensitive only to light and darkness, I was unable to tell what the girl looked like. But I knew she wore slippers from the way they slapped against her heels.

It would take me some time to discover something about her looks and perhaps I never would. But I liked the sound of her voice and even the sound of her slippers.

'Are you going all the way to Dehra?' I asked.

I must have been sitting in a dark corner because my voice startled her. She gave a little exclamation and said, 'I didn't know anyone else was here.'

Well, it often happens that people with good eyesight fail to see what is right in front of them. They have too much to take in, I suppose. Whereas people who cannot see (or see very little) have to take in only the essentials, whatever registers tellingly on their remaining senses.

'I didn't see you either,' I said. 'But I heard you come in.'

I wondered if I would be able to prevent her from discovering that I was blind. Provided I keep to my seat, I thought, it shouldn't be too difficult.

The girl said, 'I'm getting off at Saharanpur. My aunt is meeting me there.'

'Then I had better not get too familiar,' I replied. 'Aunts are usually formidable creatures.'

'Where are you going?' she asked.

'To Dehra and then to Mussoorie.'

'Oh, how lucky you are. I wish I was going to Mussoorie. I love the hills. Especially in October.'

'Yes, this is the best time,' I said, calling on my memories. 'The hills are covered with wild dahlias, the sun is delicious, and at night you can sit in front of a log fire and drink a little brandy. Most of the tourists have gone and the roads are quiet and almost deserted. Yes, October is the best time.'

She was silent. I wondered if my words had touched her or whether she thought me a romantic fool. Then I made a mistake.

'What is it like outside?' I asked.

She seemed to find nothing strange in the question. Had she noticed already that I could not see? But her next question removed my doubts.

'Why don't you look out of the window?' she asked.

I moved easily along the berth and felt for the window ledge. The window was open and I faced it, making a pretence of studying the landscape. I heard the panting of the engine, the rumble of the wheels, and, in my mind's eye I could see telegraph posts flashing by.

'Have you noticed,' I ventured, 'that the trees seem to be moving while we seem to be standing still?'

'That always happens,' she said. 'Do you see any animals?'

'No,' I answered quite confidently. I knew that there were hardly any animals left in the forests near Dehra.

I turned from the window and faced the girl, and for a while we sat in silence.

'You have an interesting face,' I remarked. I was becoming quite daring but it was a safe remark. Few girls can resist flattery. She laughed pleasantly—a clear, ringing laugh.

'It's nice to be told I have an interesting face. I'm tired of people telling me I have a pretty face.'

Oh, so you do have a pretty face, thought I. And aloud I said, 'Well, an interesting face can also be pretty.'

'You are a very gallant young man,' she said. 'But why are you so serious?'

I thought, then, that I would try to laugh for her, but the thought of laughter only made me feel troubled and lonely.

'We'll soon be at your station,' I said.

'Thank goodness it's a short journey. I can't bear to sit in a train for more than two or three hours.'

Yet, I was prepared to sit there for almost any length of time, just to listen to her talk. Her voice had the sparkle of a mountain stream. As soon as she left the train she would forget our brief encounter. But it would stay with me for the rest of the journey and for some time after.

The engine's whistle shrieked, the carriage wheels changed their sound and rhythm, the girl got up and began to collect her things. I wondered if she wore her hair in a bun or if it was plaited. Perhaps it was hanging loose over her shoulders. Or was it cut very short?

The train drew slowly into the station. Outside, there was the shouting of porters and vendors and a high-pitched female voice near the carriage door. That voice must have belonged to the girl's aunt.

'Goodbye,' the girl said.

She was standing very close to me. So close that the perfume from her hair was tantalizing. I wanted to raise my hand and touch her hair but she moved away. Only the scent of perfume still lingered where she had stood.

There was some confusion in the doorway. A man, getting into the compartment, stammered an apology. Then the door banged and the world was shut out again. I returned to my berth. The guard blew his whistle and we moved off. Once again, I had a game to play and a new fellow traveller.

The train gathered speed, the wheels took up their song, the carriage groaned and shook. I found the window and sat in front of it, staring into the daylight that was darkness for me.

So many things were happening outside the window. It could be a fascinating game guessing what went on out there.

The man who had entered the compartment broke into my reverie.

'You must be disappointed,' he said. 'I'm not nearly as attractive a travelling companion as the one who just left.'

'She was an interesting girl,' I said. 'Can you tell me—did she keep her hair long or short?'

'I don't remember,' he said, sounding puzzled. 'It was her eyes I noticed, not her hair. She had beautiful eyes, but they were of no use to her. She was completely blind. Didn't you notice?'

THE ROOM ON THE ROOF

(An Excerpt)

The afternoon was warm and lazy, unusually so for spring; very quiet, as though resting in the interval between the spring and the coming summer. There was no sign of the missionary's wife or the sweeper boy when Rusty returned, but Mr Harrison's car stood in the driveway of the house.

At the sight of the car, Rusty felt a little weak and frightened; he had not expected his guardian to return so soon and had, in fact, almost forgotten his existence. But now he forgot all about the chaat shop and Somi and Ranbir, and ran up the verandah steps in a panic.

Mr Harrison was at the top of the verandah steps, standing behind the potted palms.

The boy said, 'Oh, hullo, sir, you're back!' He knew of nothing else to say, but tried to make his little piece sound enthusiastic.

'Where have you been all day?' asked Mr Harrison, without looking once at the startled boy. 'Our neighbours haven't seen much of you lately.'

'I've been for a walk, sir.'

'You have been to the bazaar.'

The boy hesitated before making a denial; the man's eyes were on him now, and to lie Rusty would have had to lower his eyes—and this he could not do…

'Yes, sir, I went to the bazaar.'

'May I ask why?'

'Because I had nothing to do.'

'If you had nothing to do, you could have visited our neighbours. The bazaar is not the place for you. You know that.'

'But nothing happened to me...'

'That is not the point,' said Mr Harrison, and now his normally dry voice took on a faint shrill note of excitement, and he spoke rapidly. 'The point is, I have told you never to visit the bazaar. You belong here, to this house, this road, these people. Don't go where you don't belong.'

Rusty wanted to argue, longed to rebel, but fear of Mr Harrison held him back. He wanted to resist the man's authority, but he was conscious of the supple malacca cane in the glass cupboard.

'I'm sorry, sir...'

But his cowardice did him no good. The guardian went over to the glass cupboard, brought out the cane, flexed it in his hands. He said, 'It is not enough to say you are sorry, you must be made to feel sorry. Bend over the sofa.'

The boy bent over the sofa, clenched his teeth and dug his fingers into the cushions. The cane swished through the air, landing on his bottom with a slap, knocking the dust from his pants. Rusty felt no pain. But his guardian waited, allowing the cut to sink in, then he administered the second stroke, and this time it hurt, it stung into the boy's buttocks, burning up the flesh, conditioning it for the remaining cuts.

At the sixth stroke of the supple malacca cane, which was usually the last, Rusty let out a wild whoop, leapt over the sofa and charged from the room.

He lay groaning on his bed until the pain had eased.

But the flesh was so sore that he could not touch the place where the cane had fallen. Wriggling out of his pants, he examined his backside in the mirror. Mr Harrison had been most accurate:

a thick purple welt stretched across both cheeks, and a little blood trickled down the boy's thigh. The blood had a cool, almost soothing effect, but the sight of it made Rusty feel faint.

He lay down and moaned for pleasure. He pitied himself enough to want to cry, but he knew the futility of tears. But the pain and the sense of injustice he felt were both real.

A shadow fell across the bed. Someone was at the window, and Rusty looked up.

The sweeper boy showed his teeth.

'What do you want?' asked Rusty gruffly.

'You hurt, chotta sahib?'

The sweeper boy's sympathies provoked only suspicion in Rusty.

'You told Mr Harrison where I went!' said Rusty.

But the sweeper boy cocked his head to one side, and asked innocently, 'Where you went, chotta sahib?'

'Oh, never mind. Go away.'

'But you hurt?'

'Get out!' shouted Rusty.

The smile vanished, leaving only a sad frightened look in the sweeper boy's eyes.

Rusty hated hurting people's feelings, but he was not accustomed to familiarity with servants; and yet, only a few minutes ago, he had been beaten for visiting the bazaar where there were so many like the sweeper boy.

The sweeper boy turned from the window, leaving wet fingermarks on the sill; then lifted his buckets from the ground and, with his knees bent to take the weight, walked away. His feet splashed a little in the water he had spilt, and the soft red mud flew up and flecked his legs.

Angry with his guardian and with the servant and most of all with himself, Rusty buried his head in his pillow and tried to shut out reality; he forced a dream, in which he was thrashing Mr Harrison until the guardian begged for mercy.

▪

In the early morning, when it was still dark, Ranbir stopped in the jungle behind Mr Harrison's house, and slapped his drum. His thick mass of hair was covered with red dust and his body, naked but for a cloth round his waist, was smeared green; he looked like a painted god, a green god. After a minute he slapped the drum again, then sat down on his heels and waited.

Rusty woke to the sound of the second drum-beat, and lay in bed and listened; it was repeated, travelling over the still air and in through the bedroom window. *Dhum!* … A double-beat now, one deep, one high, insistent, questioning… Rusty remembered his promise, that he would play Holi with Ranbir, meet him in the jungle when he beat the drum. But he had made the promise on the condition that his guardian did not return; he could not possibly keep it now, not after the thrashing he had received.

Dhum-dhum, spoke the drum in the forest; *dhum-dhum*, impatient and getting annoyed…

'Why can't he shut up,' muttered Rusty, 'does he want to wake Mr Harrison…'

Holi, the Festival of Colours, the arrival of spring, the rebirth of the new year, the awakening of love, what were these things to him, they did not concern his life, he could not start a new life, not for one day…and besides, it all sounded very primitive, this throwing of colour and beating of drums…

Dhum-dhum!

The boy sat up in bed.

The sky had grown lighter.

From the distant bazaar came a new music, many drums and voices, faint but steady, growing in rhythm and excitement.

The sound conveyed something to Rusty, something wild and emotional, something that belonged to his dream-world, and on a sudden impulse he sprang out of bed.

He went to the door and listened; the house was quiet, he bolted the door. The colours of Holi, he knew, would stain his clothes, so he did not remove his pyjamas. In an old pair of flattened rubber-soled tennis shoes, he climbed out of the window and ran over the dew-wet grass, down the path behind the house, over the hill and into the jungle.

When Ranbir saw the boy approach, he rose from the ground. The long hand-drum, the dholak, hung at his waist. As he rose, the sun rose. But the sun did not look as fiery as Ranbir who, in Rusty's eyes, appeared as a painted demon, rather than as a god.

'You are late, mister,' said Ranbir, 'I thought you were not coming.'

He had both his fists closed, but when he walked towards Rusty he opened them, smiling widely, a white smile in a green face. In his right hand was the red dust and in his left hand the green dust. And with his right hand he rubbed the red dust on Rusty's left cheek, and then with the other hand he put the green dust on the boy's right cheek; then he stood back and looked at Rusty and laughed. Then, according to the custom, he embraced the bewildered boy. It was a wrestler's hug, and Rusty winced breathlessly.

'Come,' said Ranbir, 'let us go and make the town a rainbow.'

▪

And truly, that day there was an outbreak of spring.

The sun came up, and the bazaar woke up. The walls of the houses were suddenly patched with splashes of colour, and just as suddenly the trees seemed to have burst into flower; for in the forest there were armies of rhododendrons, and by the river the poinsettias danced; the cherry and the plum were in blossom; the snow in the mountains had melted, and the streams were rushing torrents; the new leaves on the trees were full of sweetness, the young grass held both dew and sun, and made an emerald of every dewdrop.

The infection of spring spread simultaneously through the world of man and the world of nature, and made them one.

Ranbir and Rusty moved round the hill, keeping in the fringe of the jungle until they had skirted not only the European community but also the smart shopping centre. They came down dirty little side-streets where the walls of houses, stained with the wear and tear of many years of meagre habitation, were now stained again with the vivid colours of Holi. They came to the Clock Tower.

At the Clock Tower, spring had really been declared open. Clouds of coloured dust rose in the air and spread, and jets of water—green and orange and purple, all rich emotional colours—burst out everywhere.

Children formed groups. They were armed mainly with bicycle pumps, or pumps fashioned from bamboo stems, from which was squirted liquid colour. The children paraded the main road, chanting shrilly and clapping their hands. The men and women preferred the dust to the water. They too sang, but their chanting held a significance, their hands and fingers drummed the rhythms of spring, the same rhythms, the same songs that belonged to this day every year of their lives.

Ranbir was met by some friends and greeted with great hilarity. A bicycle pump was directed at Rusty and a jet of sooty black water squirted into his face.

Blinded for a moment, Rusty blundered about in great confusion. A horde of children bore down on him, and he was subjected to a pumping from all sides. His shirt and pyjamas, drenched through, stuck to his skin; then someone gripped the end of his shirt and tugged at it until it tore and came away. Dust was thrown on the boy, on his face and body, roughly and with full force, and his tender, under-exposed skin smarted beneath the onslaught.

Then his eyes cleared. He blinked and looked wildly round at the group of boys and girls who cheered and danced in front of him. His body was running mostly with sooty black, streaked with red, and his mouth seemed full of it too, and he began to spit.

Then, one by one, Ranbir's friends approached Rusty.

Gently, they rubbed dust on the boy's cheeks, and embraced him; they were like so many flaming demons that Rusty could not distinguish one from the other. But this gentle greeting, coming so soon after the stormy bicycle-pump attack, bewildered Rusty even more.

Ranbir said, 'Now you are one of us, come,' and Rusty went with him and the others.

'Suri is hiding,' cried someone. 'He has locked himself in his house and won't play Holi!'

'Well, he will have to play,' said Ranbir, 'even if we break the house down.'

Suri, who dreaded Holi, had decided to spend the day in a state of siege; and had set up camp in his mother's kitchen, where there were provisions enough for the whole day. He listened to his playmates calling to him from the courtyard, and ignored their invitations, jeers and threats; the door was strong and well barricaded. He settled himself beneath a table, and turned the pages of the English nudists' journal, which he bought every month chiefly for its photographic value.

But the youths outside, intoxicated by the drumming and shouting and high spirits, were not going to be done out of the pleasure of discomfiting Suri. So they acquired a ladder and made their entry into the kitchen by the skylight.

Suri squealed with fright. The door was opened and he was bundled out, and his spectacles were trampled.

'My glasses!' he screamed. 'You've broken them!'

'You can afford a dozen pairs!' jeered one of his antagonists.

'But I can't see, you fools, I can't see!'

'He can't see!' cried someone in scorn. 'For once in his life, Suri can't see what's going on! Now, whenever he spies, we'll smash his glasses!'

Not knowing Suri very well, Rusty could not help pitying the frantic boy.

'Why don't you let him go?' he asked Ranbir. 'Don't force him if he doesn't want to play.'

'But this is the only chance we have of repaying him for all his dirty tricks. It is the only day on which no one is afraid of him!'

Rusty could not imagine how anyone could possibly be afraid of the pale, struggling, spindly-legged boy who was almost being torn apart, and was glad when the others had finished their sport with him.

All day Rusty roamed the town and countryside with Ranbir and his friends, and Suri was soon forgotten. For one day, Ranbir and his friends forgot their homes and their work and the problem of the next meal, and danced down the roads, out of the town and into the forest. And, for one day, Rusty forgot his guardian and the missionary's wife and the supple malacca cane, and ran with the others through the town and into the forest.

The crisp, sunny morning ripened into afternoon.

In the forest, in the cool dark silence of the jungle, they stopped singing and shouting, suddenly exhausted. They lay down in the shade of many trees, and the grass was soft and comfortable, and very soon everyone except Rusty was fast asleep.

Rusty was tired. He was hungry. He had lost his shirt and shoes, his feet were bruised, his body sore. It was only now, resting, that he noticed these things, for he had been caught up in the excitement of the colour game, overcome by an exhilaration he had never known. His fair hair was tousled and streaked with colour, and his eyes were wide with wonder.

He was exhausted now, but he was happy.

He wanted this to go on for ever, this day of feverish emotion, this life in another world. He did not want to leave the forest; it was safe, its earth soothed him, gathered him in so that the pain of his body became a pleasure...

He did not want to go home.

▪

Mr Harrison stood at the top of the verandah steps. The house was in darkness, but his cigarette glowed more brightly for it. A road lamp trapped the returning boy as he opened the gate, and Rusty knew he had been seen, but he didn't care much; if he had known that Mr Harrison had not recognized him, he would have turned back instead of walking resignedly up the garden path.

Mr Harrison did not move, nor did he appear to notice the boy's approach. It was only when Rusty climbed the verandah steps that his guardian moved and said, 'Who's that?'

Still he had not recognized the boy; and in that instant Rusty became aware of his own condition, for his body was a patchwork of paint. Wearing only torn pyjamas he could, in the half-light, have easily been mistaken for the sweeper boy or someone else's servant. It must have been a newly acquired bazaar instinct that made the boy think of escape. He turned about.

But Mr Harrison shouted, 'Come here, you!' and the tone of his voice—the tone reserved for the sweeper boy—made Rusty stop.

'Come up here!' repeated Mr Harrison.

Rusty returned to the verandah, and his guardian switched on a light; but even now there was no recognition.

'Good evening, sir,' said Rusty.

Mr Harrison received a shock. He felt a wave of anger, and then a wave of pain: was this the boy he had trained and educated—this wild, ragged, ungrateful wretch, who did not know the difference between what was proper and what was improper, what was civilized and what was barbaric, what was decent and what was shameful—and had the years of training come to nothing? Mr Harrison came out of the shadows and cursed. He brought his hand down on the back of Rusty's neck, propelled him into the drawing-room, and pushed him across the room so violently that the boy lost his balance, collided with a table and rolled over on to the ground.

Rusty looked up from the floor to find his guardian standing over him, and in the man's right hand was the supple malacca cane and the cane was twitching.

Mr Harrison's face was twitching too, it was full of fire. His lips were stitched together, sealed up with the ginger moustache, and he looked at the boy with narrowed, unblinking eyes.

'Filth!' he said, almost spitting the words in the boy's face. 'My God, what filth!'

Rusty stared fascinated at the deep yellow nicotine stains on the fingers of his guardian's raised hand. Then the wrist moved suddenly and the cane cut across the boy's face like a knife, stabbing and burning into his cheek.

Rusty cried out and cowered back against the wall; he could feel the blood trickling across his mouth. He looked round desperately for a means of escape, but the man was in front of him, over him, and the wall was behind.

Mr Harrison broke into a torrent of words. 'How can you call yourself an Englishman, how can you come back to this house in such a condition? In what gutter, in what brothel have you been! Have you seen yourself? Do you know what you look like?'

'No,' said Rusty, and for the first time he did not address his guardian as 'sir'. 'I don't care what I look like.'

'You don't...well, I'll tell you what you look like! You look like the mongrel that you are!'

'That's a lie!' exclaimed Rusty.

'It's the truth. I've tried to bring you up as an Englishman, as your father would have wished. But, as you won't have it our way, I'm telling you that he was about the only thing English about you. You're no better than the sweeper boy!'

Rusty flared into a temper, showing some spirit for the first time in his life. 'I'm no better than the sweeper boy, but I am as good as him! I'm as good as you! I'm as good as anyone!' And, instead of cringing to take the cut from the cane, he flung himself at his guardian's legs. The cane swished through the air, grazing the boy's back. Rusty wrapped his arms round his guardian's legs and pulled on them with all his strength.

Mr Harrison went over, falling flat on his back.

The suddenness of the fall must have knocked the breath from his body, because for a moment he did not move.

Rusty sprang to his feet. The cut across his face had stung him to madness, to an unreasoning hate, and he did what previously he would only have dreamt of doing. Lifting a vase of the missionary's wife's best sweet peas off the glass cupboard, he flung it at his guardian's face. It hit him on the chest, but the water and flowers flopped out over his face. He tried to get up, but he was speechless.

The look of alarm on Mr Harrison's face gave Rusty greater courage. Before the man could recover his feet and his balance, Rusty gripped him by the collar and pushed him backwards, until they both fell over on to the floor. With one hand still twisting the collar, the boy slapped his guardian's face. Mad with the pain in his own face, Rusty hit the man again and again, wildly and awkwardly, but with the giddy thrill of knowing he could do it:

he was a child no longer, he was nearly seventeen, he was a man. He could inflict pain, that was a wonderful discovery; there was a power in his body—a devil or a god—and he gained confidence in his power; and he was a man!

'Stop that, stop it!' The shout of a hysterical woman brought Rusty to his senses. He still held his guardian by the throat, but he stopped hitting him. Mr Harrison's face was very red. The missionary's wife stood in the doorway, her face white with fear. She was under the impression that Mr Harrison was being attacked by a servant or some bazaar hooligan. Rusty did not wait until she found her tongue but, with a new-found speed and agility, darted out of the drawing-room.

He made his escape from the bedroom window. From the gate he could see the missionary's wife silhouetted against the drawing-room light. He laughed out loud. The woman swivelled round and came forward a few steps. And Rusty laughed again and began running down the road to the bazaar.

▪

It was late. The smart shops and restaurants were closed. In the bazaar, oil lamps hung outside each doorway; people were asleep on the steps and platforms of shopfronts, some huddled in blankets, others rolled tight into themselves. The road, which during the day was a busy, noisy crush of people and animals, was quiet and deserted. Only a lean dog still sniffed in the gutter. A woman sang in a room high above the street—a plaintive, tremulous song—and in the far distance a jackal cried to the moon. But the empty, lifeless street was very deceptive; if the roofs could have been removed from but a handful of buildings, it would be seen that life had not really stopped but, beautiful and ugly, persisted through the night.

It was past midnight, though the Clock Tower had no way of saying it. Rusty was in the empty street, and the chaat shop was closed, a sheet of tarpaulin draped across the front. He looked up and down the road, hoping to meet someone he knew; the chaat-walla, he felt sure, would give him a blanket for the night and a place to sleep; and the next day when Somi came to meet him, he would tell his friend of his predicament, that he had run away from his guardian's house and did not intend returning. But he would have to wait till morning: the chaat shop was shuttered, barred and bolted.

He sat down on the steps, but the stone was cold and his thin cotton pyjamas offered no protection. He folded his arms and huddled up in a corner, but still he shivered. His feet were becoming numb, lifeless.

Rusty had not fully realized the hazards of the situation. He was still mad with anger and rebellion and, though the blood on his cheek had dried, his face was still smarting. He could not think clearly: the present was confusing and unreal and he could not see beyond it; what worried him was the cold and the discomfort and the pain.

The singing stopped in the high window. Rusty looked up and saw a beckoning hand. As no one else in the street showed any signs of life, Rusty got up and walked across the road until he was under the window. The woman pointed to a stairway, and he mounted it, glad of the hospitality he was being offered.

The stairway seemed to go to the stars, but it turned suddenly to lead into the woman's room. The door was slightly ajar; he knocked and a voice said, 'Come…'

The room was filled with perfume and burning incense. A musical instrument lay in one corner. The woman reclined on a bed, her hair scattered about the pillow; she had a round, pretty face, but she was losing her youth, and the fat showed in rolls at her exposed waist. She smiled at the boy, and beckoned again.

'Thank you,' said Rusty, closing the door. 'Can I sleep here?'

'Where else?' said the woman.

'Just for tonight.'

She smiled, and waited. Rusty stood in front of her, his hands behind his back.

Sit down,' she said, and patted the bedclothes beside her.

Reverently, and as respectfully as he could, Rusty sat down.

The woman ran little fair fingers over his body, and drew his head to hers; their lips were very close, almost touching, and their breathing sounded terribly loud to Rusty, but he only said, 'I am hungry.'

A poet, thought the woman, and kissed him full on the lips; but the boy drew away in embarrassment, unsure of himself, liking the woman on the bed and yet afraid of her…

'What is wrong?' she asked. 'I'm tired,' he said. The woman's friendly smile turned to a look of scorn; but she saw that he was only a boy whose eyes were full of unhappiness, and she could not help pitying him.

'You can sleep here,' she said, 'until you have lost your tiredness.'

But he shook his head. 'I will come some other time,' he said, not wishing to hurt the woman's feelings. They were both pitying each other, liking each other, but not enough to make them understand each other.

Rusty left the room. Mechanically, he descended the staircase, and walked up the bazaar road, past the silent sleeping forms, until he reached the Clock Tower. To the right of the Clock Tower was a broad stretch of grassland where, during the day, cattle grazed and children played and young men like Ranbir wrestled and kicked footballs. But now, at night, it was a vast empty space.

But the grass was soft, like the grass in the forest, and Rusty walked the length of the maidan. He found a bench and sat down, warmer for the walk. A light breeze was blowing across the maidan, pleasant and refreshing, playing with his hair. Around him everything was dark and silent and lonely. He had got away from the bazaar, which held the misery of beggars and homeless children and starving dogs, and could now concentrate on his own misery; for there was nothing like loneliness for making Rusty conscious of his unhappy state. Madness and freedom and violence were new to him: loneliness was familiar, something he understood.

Rusty was alone. Until tomorrow, he was alone for the rest of his life.

If tomorrow there was no Somi at the chaat shop, no Ranbir, then what would he do? This question badgered him persistently, making him an unwilling slave to reality. He did not know where his friends lived, he had no money, he could not ask the chaat-walla for credit on the strength of two visits. Perhaps he should return to the amorous lady in the bazaar; perhaps…but no, one thing was certain, he would never return to his guardian…

The moon had been hidden by clouds, and presently there was a drizzle. Rusty did not mind the rain, it refreshed him and made the colour run from his body; but, when it began to fall harder, he started shivering again. He felt sick. He got up, rolled his ragged pyjamas up to the thighs and crawled under the bench.

There was a hollow under the bench, and at first Rusty found it quite comfortable. But there was no grass and gradually the earth began to soften: soon he was on his hands and knees in a pool of muddy water, with the slush oozing up through his fingers and toes. Crouching there, wet and cold and muddy, he was overcome by a feeling of helplessness and self-pity: everyone and everything seemed to have turned against him; not only his people but also the bazaar and the chaat shop and even the elements. He admitted to himself that he had been too impulsive in rebelling and running away from home; perhaps there was still time to return and beg Mr Harrison's forgiveness. But could his behaviour be forgiven?

Might he not be clapped into irons for attempted murder? Most certainly he would be given another beating: not six strokes this time, but nine.

His only hope was Somi. If not Somi, then Ranbir. If not Ranbir...well, it was no use thinking further, there was no one else to think of.

The rain had ceased. Rusty crawled out from under the bench, and stretched his cramped limbs. The moon came out from a cloud and played with his wet, glistening body, and showed him the vast, naked loneliness of the maidan and his own insignificance. He longed now for the presence of people, be they beggars or women, and he broke into a trot, and the trot became a run, a frightened run, and he did not stop until he reached the Clock Tower.

THE PHOTOGRAPH

I was ten years old. My grandmother sat on the string bed under the mango tree. It was late summer and there were sunflowers in the garden and a warm wind in the trees. My grandmother was knitting a woollen scarf for the winter months. She was very old, dressed in a plain white sari. Her eyes were not very strong now, but her fingers moved quickly with the needles and the needles kept clicking all afternoon. Grandmother had white hair, but there were very few wrinkles on her skin.

I had come home after playing cricket on the maidan. I had taken my meal and now I was rummaging through a box of old books and family heirlooms that had just that day been brought out of the attic by my mother. Nothing in the box interested me very much except for a book with colourful pictures of birds and butterflies. I was going through the book, looking at the pictures, when I found a small photograph between the pages. It was a faded picture, a little yellow and foggy. It was the picture of a girl standing against a wall and behind the wall there was nothing but sky. But from the other side a pair of hands reached up, as though someone was going to climb the wall. There were flowers growing near the girl but I couldn't tell what they were. There was a creeper too but it was just a creeper.

I ran out into the garden. 'Granny!' I shouted. 'Look at this picture! I found it in the box of old things. Whose picture is it?'

I jumped on the bed beside my grandmother and she walloped me on the bottom and said, 'Now I've lost count of my stitches and the next time you do that I'll make you finish the scarf yourself.'

Granny was always threatening to teach me how to knit which I thought was a disgraceful thing for a boy to do. It was a good deterrent for keeping me out of mischief. Once I had torn the drawing-room curtains and Granny had put a needle and thread in my hand and made me stitch the curtain together, even though I made long, two-inch stitches, which had to be taken out by my mother and done again.

She took the photograph from my hand and we both stared at it for quite a long time. The girl had long, loose hair and she wore a long dress that nearly covered her ankles, and sleeves that reached her wrists, and there were a lot of bangles on her hands. But despite all this drapery, the girl appeared to be full of freedom and movement. She stood with her legs apart and her hands on her hips and had a wide, almost devilish smile on her face.

'Whose picture is it?' I asked.

'A little girl's, of course,' said Grandmother. 'Can't you tell?'

'Yes, but did you know the girl?'

'Yes, I knew her,' said Granny, 'but she was a very wicked girl and I shouldn't tell you about her. But I'll tell you about the photograph. It was taken in your grandfather's house about sixty years ago. And that's the garden wall and over the wall there was a road going to town.'

'Whose hands are they,' I asked, 'coming up from the other side?'

Grandmother squinted and looked closely at the picture, and shook her head. 'It's the first time I've noticed,' she said. 'They must have been the sweeper boy's. Or maybe they were your grandfather's.'

'They don't look like Grandfather's hands,' I said. 'His hands are all bony.'

'Yes, but this was sixty years ago.'

'Didn't he climb up the wall after the photo?'

'No, nobody climbed up. At least, I don't remember.'

'And you remember well, Granny.'

'Yes, I remember... I remember what is not in the photograph. It was a spring day and there was a cool breeze blowing, nothing like this. Those flowers at the girl's feet, they were marigolds, and the bougainvillea creeper, it was a mass of purple. You cannot see these colours in the photo and even if you could, as nowadays, you wouldn't be able to smell the flowers or feel the breeze.'

'And what about the girl?' I said. 'Tell me about the girl.'

'Well, she was a wicked girl,' said Granny. 'You don't know the trouble they had getting her into those fine clothes she's wearing.'

'I think they are terrible clothes,' I said.

'So did she. Most of the time, she hardly wore a thing. She used to go swimming in a muddy pool with a lot of ruffianly boys, and ride on the backs of buffaloes. No boy ever teased her, though, because she could kick and scratch and pull his hair out!'

'She looks like it too,' I said. 'You can tell by the way she's smiling. At any moment something's going to happen.'

'Something did happen,' said Granny. 'Her mother wouldn't let her take off the clothes afterwards, so she went swimming in them and lay for half an hour in the mud.'

I laughed heartily and Grandmother laughed too.

'Who was the girl?' I said. 'You must tell me who she was.'

'No, that wouldn't do,' said Grandmother, but I pretended I didn't know. I knew, because Grandmother still smiled in the same way, even though she didn't have as many teeth.

'Come on, Granny,' I said, 'tell me, tell me.'

But Grandmother shook her head and carried on with the knitting. And I held the photograph in my hand looking from it to my grandmother and back again, trying to find points in common between the old lady and the little pigtailed girl. A lemon-coloured butterfly settled on the end of Grandmother's knitting needle and stayed there while the needles clicked away. I made a grab at the butterfly and it flew off in a dipping flight and settled on a sunflower.

'I wonder whose hands they were,' whispered Grandmother to herself, with her head bowed, and her needles clicking away in the soft, warm silence of that summer afternoon.

THE TUNNEL

It was almost noon, and the jungle was very still, very silent. Heat waves shimmered along the railway embankment where it cut a path through the tall evergreen trees. The railway lines were two straight black serpents disappearing into the tunnel in the hillside.

Suraj stood near the cutting, waiting for the midday train. It wasn't a station, and he wasn't catching a train. He was waiting so that he could watch the steam engine come roaring out of the tunnel.

He had cycled out of Dehra and taken the jungle path until he had come to a small village. He had left the cycle there, and walked over a low scrub-covered hill and down to the tunnel exit.

Now he looked up. He had heard, in the distance, the shrill whistle of the engine. He couldn't see anything, because the train was approaching from the other side of the hill; but presently a sound like distant thunder issued from the tunnel, and he knew the train was coming through.

A second or two later, the steam engine shot out of the tunnel, snorting and puffing like some green, black and gold dragon, some beautiful monster out of Suraj's dreams. Showering sparks left and right, it roared a challenge to the jungle.

Instinctively, Suraj stepped back a few paces. Waves of hot steam struck him in the face. Even the trees seemed to flinch from the noise and heat. And then the train had gone, leaving only a plume of smoke to drift lazily over the tall shisham trees.

The jungle was still again. No one moved.

Suraj turned from his contemplation of the drifting smoke

and began walking along the embankment towards the tunnel.

The tunnel grew darker as he walked further into it. When he had gone about twenty yards it became pitch dark. Suraj had to turn and look back at the opening to reassure himself that there was still daylight outside. Ahead of him, the tunnel's other opening was just a small round circle of light.

The tunnel was still full of smoke from the train, but it would be several hours before another train came through. Till then, the cutting belonged to the jungle again.

Suraj didn't stop, because there was nothing to do in the tunnel and nothing to see. He had simply wanted to walk through, so that he would know what the inside of a tunnel was really like. The walls were damp and sticky. A bat flew past. A lizard scuttled between the lines.

Coming straight from the darkness into the light, Suraj was dazzled by the sudden glare and put a hand up to shade his eyes. He looked up at the tree-covered hillside and thought he saw something moving between the trees.

It was just a flash of orange and gold, and a long swishing tail. It was there between the trees for a second or two, and then it was gone.

About fifteen metres from the entrance to the tunnel stood the watchman's hut. Marigolds grew in front of the hut, and at the back there was a small vegetable patch. It was the watchman's duty to inspect the tunnel and keep it clear of obstacles. Every day, before the train came through, he would walk the length of the tunnel. If all was well, he would return to his hut and take a nap. If something was wrong, he would walk back up the line and wave a red flag and the engine driver would slow down. At night, the watchman lit an oil lamp and made a similar inspection of the tunnel. Of course, he would not stop the train if there was a porcupine on the line. But if there was any danger to the train, he'd go back up the line and wave his lamp to the approaching engine. If all was well, he'd hang his lamp at the door of his hut and go to sleep.

He was just settling down on his cot for an afternoon nap when he saw the boy emerge from the tunnel. He waited until Suraj was only a metre or so away and then said: 'Welcome, welcome. I don't often have visitors. Sit down for a while, and tell me why you were inspecting my tunnel.'

'Is it your tunnel?' asked Suraj.

'It is,' said the watchman. 'It is truly my tunnel, since no one else will have anything to do with it. I have only lent it to the Government.'

Suraj sat down on the edge of the cot.

'I wanted to see the train come through,' he said. 'And then, when it had gone, I thought I'd walk through the tunnel.'

'And what did you find in it?'

'Nothing. It was very dark. But when I came out, I thought I saw an animal—up on the hill—but I'm not sure, it moved off very quickly.'

'It was a leopard you saw,' said the watchman. 'My leopard.'

'Do you own a leopard too?'

'I do.'

'And do you lend it to the Government?'

'I do not.'

'Is it dangerous?'

'No, it's a leopard that minds its own business. It comes to this range for a few days every month.'

'Have you been here a long time?' asked Suraj.

'Many years. My name is Sunder Singh.'

'My name's Suraj.'

'There is one train during the day. And there is one train during the night. Have you seen the night mail come through the tunnel?'

'No. At what time does it come?'

'About nine o'clock, if it isn't late. You could come and sit here with me, if you like. And after it has gone, instead of going to sleep I will take you home.'

'I'll ask my parents,' said Suraj. 'Will it be safe?'

'Of course. It is safer in the jungle than in the town. Nothing happens to me out here. But last month, when I went into town, I was almost run over by a bus.'

Sunder Singh yawned and stretched himself out on the cot. 'And now I am going to take a nap, my friend. It is too hot to be up and about in the afternoon.'

'Everyone goes to sleep in the afternoon,' complained Suraj. 'My father lies down as soon as he's had his lunch.'

'Well, the animals also rest in the heat of the day. It is only the tribe of boys who cannot, or will not, rest.'

Sunder Singh placed a large banana leaf over his face to keep away the flies, and was soon snoring gently. Suraj stood up, looking up and down the railway tracks. Then he began walking back to the village.

The following evening, towards dusk, as the flying foxes swooped silently out of the trees, Suraj made his way to the watchman's hut.

It had been a long hot day, but now the earth was cooling, and a light breeze was moving through the trees. It carried with it the scent of mango blossoms, the promise of rain.

Sunder Singh was waiting for Suraj. He had watered his small garden, and the flowers looked cool and fresh. A kettle was boiling on a small oil stove.

'I am making tea,' he said. 'There is nothing like a glass of hot tea while waiting for a train.'

They drank their tea, listening to the sharp notes of the tailorbird and the noisy chatter of the seven sisters.

As the brief twilight faded, most of the birds fell silent. Sunder Singh lit his oil lamp and said it was time for him to inspect the tunnel. He moved off towards the tunnel, while Suraj sat on the cot, sipping his tea. In the dark, the trees seemed to move closer to him. And the nightlife of the forest was conveyed on the breeze—the sharp call of a barking deer, the cry of a fox, the quaint *tonk-tonk* of a nightjar. There were some sounds that Suraj didn't recognize—sounds that came from the trees, creakings and whisperings, as though the trees were coming to life, stretching their limbs in the dark, shifting a little, flexing their fingers.

Sunder Singh stood inside the tunnel, trimming his lamp. The night sounds were familiar to him and he did not give them much thought; but something else—a padded footfall, a rustle of dry leaves—made him stand still for a few seconds, peering into the darkness. Then, humming softly to himself, he returned to where Suraj was waiting. Ten minutes remained for the night mail to arrive.

As Sunder Singh sat down on the cot beside Suraj, a new sound reached both of them quite distinctly—a rhythmic sawing sound, as of someone cutting through the branch of a tree.

'What's that?' whispered Suraj.

'It's the leopard,' said Sunder Singh. 'I think it's in the tunnel.'

'The train will soon be here,' said Suraj.

'Yes, my friend. And if we don't drive the leopard out of the tunnel, it will be run over and killed. I can't let that happen.'

'But won't it attack us if we try to drive it out?' asked Suraj, beginning to share the watchman's concern.

'Not this leopard. It knows me well. We have seen each other many times. It has a weakness for goats and stray dogs, but it will not harm us. Even so, I'll take my axe with me. You stay here, Suraj.'

'No, I'm coming with you. It will be better than sitting here alone in the dark!'

'All right, but stay close behind me. And remember, there is nothing to fear.'

Raising his lamp, Sunder Singh advanced into the tunnel, shouting at the top of his voice to try and scare away the animal. Suraj followed close behind; but he found he was unable to do any shouting. His throat was quite dry.

They had gone about twenty paces into the tunnel when the light from the lamp fell upon the leopard. It was crouching between the tracks, only five metres away from them. It was not a very big leopard, but it looked lithe and sinewy. Baring its teeth and snarling, it went down on its belly, tail twitching.

Suraj and Sunder Singh both shouted together. Their voices rang through the tunnel. And the leopard, uncertain as to how many terrifying humans were there in the tunnel with him, turned swiftly and disappeared into the darkness.

To make sure that it had gone, Sunder Singh and Suraj walked the length of the tunnel. When they returned to the entrance, the rails were beginning to hum. They knew the train was coming.

Suraj put his hand to one of the rails and felt its tremor. He heard the distant rumble of the train. And then the engine came round the bend, hissing at them, scattering sparks into the darkness, defying the jungle as it roared through the steep sides of the cutting. It charged straight at the tunnel, and into it, thundering past Suraj like the beautiful dragon of his dreams.

And when it had gone, the silence returned and the forest seemed to breathe, to live again. Only the rails still trembled with the passing of the train.

They trembled again to the passing of the same train, almost a week later, when Suraj and his father were both travelling in it.

Suraj's father was scribbling in a notebook, doing his accounts. Suraj sat at an open window staring out at the darkness. His father was going to Delhi on a business trip and had decided to take the boy along. ('I don't know where he gets to, most of the time,' he'd complained. 'I think it's time he learnt something about my business.')

The night mail rushed through the forest with its hundreds of passengers. The carriage wheels beat out a steady rhythm on the rails. Tiny flickering lights came and went, as they passed small villages on the fringe of the jungle.

Suraj heard the rumble as the train passed over a small bridge. It was too dark to see the hut near the cutting, but he knew they must be approaching the tunnel. He strained his eyes looking out into the night; and then, just as the engine let out a shrill whistle, Suraj saw the lamp.

He couldn't see Sunder Singh, but he saw the lamp, and he knew that his friend was out there.

The train went into the tunnel and out again; it left the jungle behind and thundered across the endless plains.

Suraj stared out at the darkness, thinking of the lonely cutting in the forest and the watchman with the lamp who would always remain a firefly for those travelling thousands as he lit up the darkness for steam engines and leopards.

BOYHOOD DREAMS

> You must pass your exams and go to college, but do not feel that if you fail, you will be able to do nothing.

My room in Shahganj was very small. I had paced about in it so often that I knew its exact measurements: twelve feet by ten. The string of my cot needed tightening. The dip in the middle was so pronounced that I invariably woke up in the morning with a backache; but I was hopeless at tightening charpoy strings.

Under the cot was my tin trunk. Its contents ranged from old, rejected manuscripts to clothes and letters and photographs. I had resolved that one day, when I had made some money with a book, I would throw the trunk and everything else out of the window, and leave Shahganj forever. But until then I was a prisoner. The rent was nominal, the window had a view of the bus stop and rickshaw stand, and I had nowhere else to go.

I did not live entirely alone. Sometimes a beggar spent the night on the balcony; and, during cold or wet weather, the boys from the tea shop, who normally slept on the pavement, crowded into the room.

Usually I woke early in the mornings, as sleep was fitful, uneasy, crowded with dreams. I knew it was five o'clock when I heard the first upcountry bus leaving its shed. I would then get up and take a walk in the fields beyond the railroad tracks.

One morning, while I was walking in the fields, I noticed someone lying across the pathway, his head and shoulders hidden by the stalks of young sugar cane. When I came near, I saw he was a boy of about sixteen. His body was twitching convulsively, his face was very white, except where a little blood had trickled down his chin. His legs kept moving and his hands fluttered restlessly, helplessly.

'What's the matter with you?' I asked, kneeling down beside him.

But he was still unconscious and could not answer me.

I ran down the footpath to a well and, dipping the end of my shirt in a shallow trough of water, ran back and sponged the boy's face. The twitching ceased and, though he still breathed heavily, his hands became still and his face calm. He opened his eyes and stared at me without any immediate comprehension.

'You have bitten your tongue,' I said, wiping the blood from his mouth. 'Don't worry. I'll stay with you until you feel better.'

He sat up now and said, 'I'm all right, thank you.'

'What happened?' I asked, sitting down beside him.

'Oh, nothing much. It often happens, I don't know why. But I cannot control it.'

'Have you seen a doctor?'

'I went to the hospital in the beginning. They gave me some pills, which I had to take every day. But the pills made me so tired and sleepy that I couldn't work properly. So I stopped taking them. Now this happens once or twice a month. But what does it matter? I'm all right when it's over, and I don't feel anything while it is happening.'

He got to his feet, dusting his clothes and smiling at me. He was slim, long-limbed and bony. There was a little fluff on his cheeks and the promise of a moustache.

'Where do you live?' I asked. 'I'll walk back with you.'

'I don't live anywhere,' he said. 'Sometimes I sleep in the temple, sometimes in the gurdwara. In summer months I sleep in the municipal gardens.'

'Well, then let me come with you as far as the gardens.'

He told me that his name was Kamal, that he studied at the Shahganj High School, and that he hoped to pass his examinations in a few months' time. He was studying hard and, if he passed with a good division, he hoped to attend a college. If he failed, there was only the prospect of continuing to live in the municipal gardens...

He carried with him a small tray of merchandise, supported by straps that went round his shoulders. In it were combs and buttons and cheap toys and little vials of perfume. All day he walked about Shahganj, selling odds and ends to people in the bazaar or at their houses. He made, on an average, two rupees a day, which was enough for his food and his school fees.

He told me all this while we walked back to the bus stand. I returned to my room, to try and write something, while Kamal went on to the bazaar to try and sell his wares.

There was nothing very unusual about Kamal's being an orphan and a refugee. During the communal holocaust of 1947, thousands of homes had been broken up, and women and children had been killed. What was unusual in Kamal was his sensitivity, a quality I thought rare in a Punjabi youth who had grown up in the Frontier Provinces during a period of hate and violence. And it was not so much his positive attitude to life that appealed to me (most people in Shahganj were completely resigned to their lot) as his gentleness, his quiet voice and the smile that flickered across his face regardless of whether he was sad or happy. In the morning, when I opened my door, I found Kamal asleep at the top of the steps. His tray lay a few feet away. I shook him gently, and he woke at once.

'Have you been sleeping here all night?' I asked. 'Why didn't you come inside?'

'It was very late,' he said. 'I didn't want to disturb you.'

'Someone could have stolen your things while you slept.'

'Oh, I sleep quite lightly. Besides, I have nothing of special value. But I came to ask you something.'

'Do you need any money?'

'No. I want you to take your meal with me tonight.'

'But where? You don't have a place of your own. It will be too expensive in a restaurant.'

'In your room,' said Kamal. 'I will bring the food and cook it here. You have a stove?'

'I think so,' I said. 'I will have to look for it.'

'I will come at seven,' said Kamal, strapping on his tray. 'Don't worry. I know how to cook!'

He ran down the steps and made for the bazaar. I began to look for the oil stove, found it at the bottom of my tin trunk, and then discovered I hadn't any pots or pans or dishes. Finally, I borrowed these from Deep Chand, the barber.

Kamal brought a chicken for our dinner. This was a costly luxury in Shahganj, to be taken only two or three times a year. He had bought the bird for three rupees, which was cheap, considering it was not too skinny. While Kamal set about roasting it, I went down to the bazaar and procured a bottle of beer on credit, and this served as an appetizer.

'We are having an expensive meal,' I observed. 'Three rupees for the chicken and three rupees for the beer. But I wish we could do it more often.'

'We should do it at least once a month,' said Kamal. 'It should be possible if we work hard.'

'You know how to work. You work from morning to night.'

'But you are a writer, Rusty. That is different. You have to wait for a mood.'

'Oh, I'm not a genius that I can afford the luxury of moods. No, I'm just lazy, that's all.'

'Perhaps you are writing the wrong things.'

'I know I am. But I don't know how I can write anything else.'

'Have you tried?'

'Yes, but there is no money in it. I wish I could make a living in some other way. Even if I repaired cycles, I would make more money.'

'Then why not repair cycles?'

'No, I will not repair cycles. I would rather be a bad writer than a good repairer of cycles. But let us not think of work. There is time enough for work. I want to know more about you.'

Kamal did not know if his parents were alive or dead. He had lost them, literally, when he was six. It happened at the Amritsar railroad station, where trains coming across the border disgorged thousands of refugees, or pulled into the station half empty, drenched with blood and littered with corpses.

Kamal and his parents were lucky to escape the massacre. Had they travelled on an earlier train (they had tried desperately to get into one), they might well have been killed; but circumstances favoured them then, only to trick them later.

Kamal was clinging to his mother's sari, while she remained close to her husband, who was elbowing his way through the frightened, bewildered throng of refugees. Glancing over his shoulder at a woman who lay on the ground, wailing and beating her breasts, Kamal collided with a burly Sikh and lost his grip on his mother's sari.

The Sikh had a long curved sword at his waist; and Kamal stared up at him in awe and fascination—at his long hair, which had fallen loose, and his wild black beard, and the bloodstains on his white shirt. The Sikh pushed him out of the way and when Kamal looked around for his mother, she was not to be seen. She was hidden from him by a mass of restless bodies, pushed in different directions. He could hear her calling, 'Kamal, where are you, Kamal?' He tried to force his way through the crowd, in the direction of the voice, but he was carried the other way…

At night, when the platform was empty, he was still searching for his mother. Eventually, some soldiers took him away. They looked for his parents, but without success, and finally, they sent Kamal to a refugee camp. From there he went to an orphanage. But when he was eight, and felt himself a man, he ran away.

He worked for some time as a helper in a tea shop; but, when he started getting epileptic fits, the shopkeeper asked him to leave, and he found himself on the streets, begging for a living. He begged for a year, moving from one town to another, and ended up finally at Shahganj. By then he was twelve and too old to beg; but he had saved some money, and with it he bought a small stock of combs, buttons, cheap perfumes and bangles; and, converting himself into a mobile shop, went from door to door, selling his wares.

Shahganj was a small town, and there was no house which Kamal hadn't visited. Everyone recognized him, and there were some who offered him food and drink; the children knew him well, because he played a small flute whenever he made his rounds, and they followed him to listen to the flute.

I began to look forward to Kamal's presence. He dispelled some of my own loneliness. I found I could work better, knowing that I did not have to work alone. And Kamal came to me, perhaps because I was the first person to have taken a personal interest in his life, and because I saw nothing frightening in his sickness. Most people in Shahganj thought epilepsy was infectious; some considered it a form of divine punishment for sins committed in a former life. Except for children, those who knew of his condition generally gave him a wide berth.

At sixteen, a boy grows like young wheat, springing up so fast that he is unaware of what is taking place within him. His mind quickens, his gestures become more confident. Hair sprouts like young grass on his face and chest, and his muscles begin to mature. Never again will he experience so much change and growth in so short a time. He is full of currents and countercurrents.

Kamal combined the bloom of youth with the beauty of the short-lived. It made me sad even to look at his pale, slim body. It hurt me to look into his eyes. Life and death were always struggling in their depths.

'Should I go to Delhi and take up a job?' I asked.

'Why not? You are always talking about it.'

'Why don't you come, too? Perhaps they can stop your fits.'

'We will need money for that. When I have passed my examinations, I will come.'

'Then I will wait,' I said. I was twenty-two, and there was world enough and time for everything.

We decided to save a little money from his small earnings and my occasional payments. We would need money to go to Delhi, money to live there until we could earn a living. We put away twenty rupees one week, but lost it the next when we lent it to a friend who owned a cycle rickshaw. But this gave us the occasional use of his cycle rickshaw, and early one morning, with Kamal sitting on the crossbar, I rode out of Shahganj.

After cycling for about two miles, we got down and pushed the cycle off the road, taking a path through a paddy field and then through a field of young maize, until in the distance we saw a tree, a crooked tree, growing beside an old well.

I do not know the name of that tree. I had never seen one like it before. It had a crooked trunk and crooked branches, and was clothed in thick, broad, crooked leaves, like the leaves on which food is served in the bazaar.

In the trunk of the tree there was a hole, and when we set the bicycle down with a crash, a pair of green parrots flew out, and went dipping and swerving across the fields. There was grass around the well, cropped short by grazing cattle.

We sat in the shade of the crooked tree, and Kamal untied the red cloth in which he had brought our food. When we had eaten, we stretched ourselves out on the grass. I closed my eyes and became aware of a score of different sensations. I heard a cricket singing in the tree, the cooing of pigeons from the walls of the old well, the quiet breathing of Kamal, the parrots returning to the tree, the distant hum of an airplane. I smelled the grass and the old bricks round the well and the promise of rain. I felt Kamal's fingers against my arm, and the sun creeping over my cheek. And when I opened my eyes, there were clouds on the horizon, and Kamal was asleep, his arm thrown across his face to keep out the glare.

I went to the well, and putting my shoulders to the ancient handle, turned the wheel, moving it around while cool, clean water gushed out over the stones and along the channel to the fields. The discovery that I could water a field, that I had the power to make things grow, gave me a thrill of satisfaction; it was like writing a story that had the ring of truth. I drank from one of the trays; the water was sweet with age.

Kamal was sitting up, looking at the sky.

'It's going to rain,' he said.

We began cycling homeward; but we were still some way out of Shahganj when it began to rain. A lashing wind swept the rain across our faces, but we exulted in it, and sang at the top of our voices until we reached the Shahganj bus stop.

Across the railroad tracks and the dry riverbed, fields of maize stretched away, until there came a dry region of thorn bushes and lantana scrub, where the earth was cut into jagged cracks, like a jigsaw puzzle. Dotting the landscape were old, abandoned brick kilns. When it rained heavily, the hollows filled up with water.

Kamal and I came to one of these hollows to bathe and swim. There was an island in the middle of it, and on this small mound lay the ruins of a hut where a nightwatchman had once lived, looking after the brick kilns. We would swim out to the island, which was only a few yards from the banks of the hollow. There was a grassy patch in front of the hut, and early in the mornings, before it got too hot, we would wrestle on the grass.

Though I was heavier than Kamal, my chest as sound as a new drum, he had strong, wiry arms and legs, and would often pinion me around the waist with his bony knees. Now, while we wrestled on the new monsoon grass, I felt his body go tense. He stiffened, his legs jerked against my body, and a shudder passed through him. I knew that he had a fit coming on, but I was unable to extricate myself from his arms.

He gripped me more tightly as the fit took possession of him. Instead of struggling, I lay still, tried to absorb some of his anguish, tried to draw some of his agitation to myself. I had a strange fancy that by identifying myself with his convulsions, I might alleviate them.

I pressed against Kamal, and whispered soothingly into his ear; and then, when I noticed his mouth working, I thrust my fingers between his teeth to prevent him from biting his tongue. But so violent was the convulsion that his teeth bit into the flesh of my palm and ground against my knuckles. I shouted with the pain and tried to jerk my hand away, but it was impossible to loosen the grip of his jaws. So I closed my eyes and counted—counted till seven—until consciousness returned to him and his muscles relaxed.

My hand was shaking and covered with blood. I bound it in my handkerchief and kept it hidden from Kamal.

We walked back to the room without talking much. Kamal looked depressed and weak. I kept my hand beneath my shirt, and Kamal was too dejected to notice anything. It was only at night, when he returned from his classes, that he noticed the cuts, and I told him I had slipped in the road, cutting my hand on some broken glass.

Rain upon Shahganj. And, until the rain stops, Shahganj is fresh and clean and alive. The children run out of their houses, glorying in their nakedness. The gutters choke, and the narrow street becomes a torrent of water, coursing merrily down to the bus stop. It swirls over the trees and the roofs of the town, and the parched earth soaks it up, exuding a fragrance that comes only once in a year, the fragrance of quenched earth, that most exhilarating of smells.

The rain swept in through the door and soaked the cot. When I had succeeded in closing the door, I found the roof leaking, the water trickling down the walls and forming new pictures on the cracking plaster. The door flew open again, and there was Kamal standing on the threshold, shaking himself like a wet dog. Coming in, he stripped and dried himself, and then sat shivering on the bed while I made frantic efforts to close the door again.

'You need some tea,' I said.

He nodded, forgetting to smile for once, and I knew his mind was elsewhere, in one of a hundred possible places from his dreams.

'One day I will write a book,' I said, as we drank strong tea in the fast-fading twilight. 'A real book, about real people. Perhaps it will be about you and me and Shahganj. And then we will run away from Shahganj, fly on the wings of Garuda, and all our troubles will be over and fresh troubles will begin. Why should we mind difficulties, as long as they are new difficulties?'

'First I must pass my exams,' said Kamal. 'Otherwise, I can do nothing, go nowhere.'

'Don't take exams too seriously. I know that in India they are the passport to any kind of job, and that you cannot become a clerk unless you have a degree. But do not forget that you are studying for the sake of acquiring knowledge, and not for the sake of becoming a clerk. You don't want to become a clerk or a bus conductor, do you? You must pass your exams and go to college, but do not feel that if you fail, you will be able to do nothing. Why, you can start making your own buttons instead of selling other people's!'

'You are right,' said Kamal. 'But why not be an educated button manufacturer?'

'Why not, indeed? That's just what I mean. And, while you are studying for your exams, I will be writing my book. I will start tonight! It is an auspicious night, the beginning of the monsoon.'

The light did not come on. A tree must have fallen across the wires. I lit a candle and placed it on the windowsill and, while the candle spluttered in the steamy air, Kamal opened his books and, with one hand on a book and the other hand playing with his toes—this attitude helped him to concentrate—he devoted his attention to algebra.

I took an ink bottle down from a shelf and, finding it empty, added a little rainwater to the crusted contents. Then I sat down beside Kamal and began to write; but the pen was useless and made blotches all over the paper, and I had no idea what I should write about, though I was full of writing just then. So I began to look at Kamal instead; at his eyes, hidden in shadow, and his hands, quiet in the candlelight; and I followed his breathing and the slight movement of his lips as he read softly to himself.

And, instead of starting my book, I sat and watched Kamal.

Sometimes Kamal played the flute at night, while I was lying awake; and, even when I was asleep, the flute would play in my dreams. Sometimes he brought it to the crooked tree, and played it for the benefit of the birds; but the parrots only made harsh noises and flew away.

Once, when Kamal was playing his flute to a group of children, he had a fit. The flute fell from his hands, and he began to roll about in the dust on the roadside. The children were frightened and ran away. But the next time they heard Kamal play his flute, they came to listen as usual.

That Kamal was gaining in strength I knew from the way he was able to pin me down whenever we wrestled on the grass near the old brick kilns. It was no longer necessary for me to yield deliberately to him. And, though his fits still recurred from time to time—as we knew they would continue to do—he was not so depressed afterwards. The anxiety and the death had gone from his eyes.

His examinations were nearing, and he was working hard. (I had yet to begin the first chapter of my book.) Because of the necessity of selling two or three rupees' worth of articles every day, he did not get much time for studying; but he stuck to his books until past midnight, and it was seldom that I heard his flute.

He put aside his tray of odds and ends during the examinations, and walked to the examination centre instead. And after two weeks, when it was all over, he took up his tray and began his rounds again. In a burst of creativity, I wrote three pages of my novel.

On the morning the results of the examination were due, I rose early, before Kamal, and went down to the news agency. It was five o'clock and the newspapers had just arrived. I went through the columns relating to Shahganj, but I couldn't find Kamal's roll number on the list of successful candidates. I had the number written down on a slip of paper, and I looked at it again to make sure that I had compared it correctly with the others; then I went through the newspaper once more.

When I returned to the room, Kamal was sitting on the doorstep. I didn't have to tell him he had failed. He knew by the look on my face. I sat down beside him, and we said nothing for some time.

'Never mind,' said Kamal, eventually. 'I will pass next year.'

I realized that I was more depressed than he was, and that he was trying to console me.

'If only you'd had more time,' I said.

'I have plenty of time now. Another year. And you will have time in which to finish your book; then we can both go away. Another year of Shahganj won't be so bad. As long as I have your friendship, almost everything else can be tolerated, even my sickness.'

And then, turning to me with an expression of intense happiness, he said, 'Yesterday I was sad, and tomorrow I may be sad again, but today I know that I am happy. I want to live on and on. I feel that life isn't long enough to satisfy me.'

He stood up, the tray hanging from his shoulders.

'What would you like to buy?' he said. 'I have everything you need.'

At the bottom of the steps he turned and smiled at me, and I knew then that I had written my story.

THE THIEF'S STORY

I was still a thief when I met Romi. And though I was only fifteen years old, I was an experienced and fairly successful hand. Romi was watching a wrestling match when I approached him. He was about twenty-five and he looked easy-going, kind, and simple enough for my purpose. I was sure I would be able to win the young man's confidence.

'You look a bit of a wrestler yourself,' I said. There's nothing like flattery to break the ice!

'So do you,' he replied, which put me off for a moment because at that time I was rather thin and bony.

Well,' I said modestly, 'I do wrestle a bit.'

What's your name?'

'Hari Singh,' I lied. I took a new name every month, which kept me ahead of the police and former employers.

After these formalities Romi confined himself to commenting on the wrestlers, who were grunting, gasping and heaving each other about. When he walked away, I followed him casually.

'Hello again,' he said.

I gave him my most appealing smile. 'I want to work for you,' I said.

'But I can't pay you anything—not for some time, anyway.'

I thought that over for a minute. Perhaps I had misjudged my man. 'Can you feed me?' I asked.

'Can you cook?'

'I can cook,' I lied again.

'If you can cook, then maybe I can feed you.'

He took me to his room over the Delhi Sweet Shop and told me I could sleep on the balcony. But the meal I cooked that night must have been terrible because Romi gave it to a stray dog and told me to be off.

But I just hung around, smiling in my most appealing way, and he couldn't help laughing.

Later, he said never mind, he'd teach me to cook. He also taught me to write my name and said he would soon teach me to write whole sentences and to add figures. I was grateful. I knew that once I could write like an educated person, there would be no limit to what I could achieve.

It was quite pleasant working for Romi. I made tea in the morning and then took my time buying the day's supplies, usually making a profit of two or three rupees. I think he knew I made a little money this way, but he didn't seem to mind.

Romi made money by fits and starts. He would borrow one week, lend the next. He kept worrying about his next cheque, but as soon as it arrived he would go out and celebrate. He wrote for the *Delhi* and *Bombay* magazines: a strange way to make a living.

One evening he came home with a small bundle of notes, saying he had just sold a book to a publisher. That night I saw him put the money in an envelope and tuck it under the mattress.

I had been working for Romi for almost a month and, apart from cheating on the shopping, had not done anything big in my real line of work. I had every opportunity for doing so. I could come and go as I pleased, and Romi was the most trusting person I had ever met.

That was why it was so difficult to rob him. It was easy for me to rob a greedy man. But robbing a nice man could be a problem. And if he doesn't notice he's being robbed, then all the spice goes out of the undertaking!

Well, it's time I got down to some real work, I told myself. If

I don't take the money, he'll only waste it on his so-called friends. After all, he doesn't even give me a salary.

Romi was sleeping peacefully. A beam of moonlight reached over the balcony and fell on his bed. I sat on the floor, considering the situation. If I took the money, I could catch the 10.30 express to Lucknow. Slipping out of my blanket, I crept over to the bed.

My hand slid under the mattress, searching for the notes. When I found the packet, I drew it out without a sound. Romi sighed in his sleep and turned on his side. Startled, I moved quickly out of the room.

Once on the road, I began to run. I had the money stuffed into a vest pocket under my shirt. When I'd gotten some distance from Romi's place, I slowed to a walk and, taking the envelope from my pocket, counted the money. Seven hundred rupees in fifties. I could live like a prince for a week or two!

When I reached the station, I did not stop at the ticket office (I had never bought a ticket in my life) but dashed straight on to the platform. The Lucknow Express was just moving out. The train had still to pick up speed and I should have been able to jump into one of the compartments, but I hesitated—for some reason I can't explain—and I lost the chance to get away.

When the train had gone, I found myself standing alone on the deserted platform. I had no idea where to spend the night. I had no friends, believing that friends were more trouble than help. And I did not want to arouse curiosity by staying at one of the small hotels nearby. The only person I knew really well was the man I had robbed. Leaving the station, I walked slowly through the bazaar.

In my short career, I had made a study of people's faces after they had discovered the loss of their valuables. The greedy showed panic; the rich showed anger; the poor, resignation. But I knew that Romi's face when he discovered the theft would show only a touch of sadness—not for the loss of money, but for the loss of trust.

The night was chilly—November nights can be cold in northern India—and a shower of rain added to my discomfort. I sat down in the shelter of the clock tower. A few beggars and vagrants lay beside me, rolled up tight in their blankets. The clock showed midnight. I felt for the notes; they were soaked through.

Romi's money. In the morning, he would probably have given me five rupees to go to the movies, but now I had it all: no more cooking meals, running to the bazaar or learning to write sentences.

Sentences! I had forgotten about them in the excitement of the theft. Writing complete sentences, I knew, could one day bring me more than a few hundred rupees. It was a simple matter to steal. But to be a really big man, a clever and respected man, was something else. I should go back to Romi, I told myself, if only to learn to read and write.

I hurried back to the room feeling very nervous, for it is much easier to steal something than to return it undetected.

I opened the door quietly, then stood in the doorway in clouded moonlight. Romi was still asleep. I crept to the head of the bed, and my hand came up with the packet of notes. I felt his breath on my hand. I remained still for a few moments. Then my fingers found the edge of the mattress, and I slipped the money beneath it.

I awoke late the next morning to find that Romi had already made the tea. He stretched out a hand to me. There was a fifty-rupee note between his fingers. My heart sank.

'I made some money yesterday,' he said. 'Now I'll be able to pay you regularly.'

My spirits rose. But when I took the note, I noticed that it was still wet from the night's rain.

So he knew what I'd done. But neither his lips nor his eyes revealed anything.

'Today we'll start writing sentences,' he said.

I smiled at Romi in my most appealing way. And the smile came by itself, without any effort.

LOVE IS A SAD SONG

I sit against this grey rock, beneath a sky of pristine blueness, and think of you, Sushila. It is November and the grass is turning brown and yellow. Crushed, it still smells sweet. The afternoon sun shimmers on the oak leaves and turns them a glittering silver. A cricket sizzles its way through the long grass. The stream murmurs at the bottom of the hill—that stream where you and I lingered on a golden afternoon in May.

I sit here and think of you and try to see your slim brown hand resting against this rock, feeling its warmth. I am aware again of the texture of your skin, the coolness of your feet, the sharp tingle of your fingertips. And in the pastures of my mind I run my hand over your quivering mouth and crush your tender breasts. Remembered passion grows sweeter with the passing of time.

You will not be thinking of me now, as you sit in your home in the city, cooking or sewing or trying to study for examinations. There will be men and women and children circling about you, in that crowded house of your grandmother's, and you will not be able to think of me for more than a moment or two. But I know you do think of me sometimes, in some private moment which cuts you off from the crowd. You will remember how I wondered what it is all about, this loving, and why it should cause such an upheaval. You are still a child, Sushila—and yet you found it so easy to quieten my impatient heart.

On the night you came to stay with us, the light from the street lamp shone through the branches of the peach tree and made leaf patterns on the walls. Through the glass panes of the front door

I caught a glimpse of little Sunil's face, bright and questing, and then—a hand—a dark, long-fingered hand that could only have belonged to you.

It was almost a year since I had seen you, my dark and slender girl. And now you were in your sixteenth year. And Sunil was twelve; and your uncle, Dinesh, who lived with me, was twenty-three. And I was almost thirty—a fearful and wonderful age, when life becomes dangerous for dreamers.

I remember that when I left Delhi last year, you cried. At first I thought it was because I was going away. Then I realized that it was because you could not go anywhere yourself. Did you envy my freedom—the freedom to live in a poverty of my own choosing, the freedom of the writer? Sunil, to my surprise, did not show much emotion at my going away. This hurt me a little, because during that year he had been particularly close to me, and I felt for him a very special love. But separations cannot be of any significance to small boys of twelve who live for today, tomorrow, and—if they are very serious—the day after.

Before I went away with Dinesh, you made us garlands of marigolds. They were orange and gold, fresh and clean and kissed by the sun. You garlanded me as I sat talking to Sunil. I remember you both as you looked that day—Sunil's smile dimpling his cheeks, while you gazed at me very seriously, your expression very tender. I loved you even then…

Our first picnic.

The path to the little stream took us through the oak forest, where the flashy blue magpies played follow-my-leader with their harsh, creaky calls. Skirting an open ridge (the place where I now sit and write), the path dipped through oak, rhododendron and maple, until it reached a little knoll above the stream. It was a spot unknown to the tourists and summer visitors. Sometimes a milkman or woodcutter crossed the stream on the way to town or village but no one lived beside it. Wild roses grew on the banks.

I do not remember much of that picnic. There was a lot of dull conversation with our neighbours, the Kapoors, who had come along too. You and Sunil were rather bored. Dinesh looked preoccupied. He was fed up with college. He wanted to start earning a living: wanted to paint. His restlessness often made him moody, irritable.

Near the knoll the stream was too shallow for bathing, but I told Sunil about a cave and a pool further downstream and promised that we would visit the pool another day.

That same night, after dinner, we took a walk along the dark road that goes past the house and leads to the burning ghat. Sunil, who had already sensed the intimacy between us, took my hand and put it in yours. An odd, touching little gesture!

'Tell us a story,' you said.

'Yes, tell us,' said Sunil.

I told you the story of the pure in heart. A shepherd boy found a snake in the forest and the snake told the boy that it was really a princess who had been bewitched and turned into a snake, and that it could only recover its human form if someone who was truly pure in heart gave it three kisses on the mouth. The boy put his lips to the mouth of the snake and kissed it thrice. And the snake was transformed into a beautiful princess. But the boy lay cold and dead.

'You always tell sad stories,' complained Sunil.

'I like sad stories,' you said. 'Tell us another.'

'Tomorrow night. I'm sleepy.'

We were woken in the night by a strong wind which went whistling round the old house and came rushing down the chimney, humming and hawing and finally choking itself.

Sunil woke up and cried out, 'What's that noise, Uncle?'

'Only the wind,' I said.

'Not a ghost?'

'Well, perhaps the wind is made up of ghosts. Perhaps this wind contains the ghosts of all the people who have lived and died in this old house and want to come in again from the cold.'

You told me about a boy who had been fond of you in Delhi. Apparently he had visited the house on a few occasions, and had sometimes met you on the street while you were on your way home from school. At first, he had been fond of another girl but later he switched his affections to you. When you told me that he had written to you recently, and that before coming up you had replied to his letter, I was consumed by jealousy—an emotion which I thought I had grown out of long ago. It did not help to be told that you were not serious about the boy, that you were sorry for him because he had already been disappointed in love.

'If you feel sorry for everyone who has been disappointed in love,' I said, 'you will soon be receiving the affections of every young man over ten.'

'Let them give me their affections,' you said, 'and I will give them my chappal over their heads.'

'But spare my head,' I said.

'Have you been in love before?'

'Many times. But this is the first time.'

'And who is your love?'

'Haven't you guessed?'

Sunil, who was following our conversation with deep interest, seemed to revel in the situation. Probably he fancied himself playing the part of Cupid, or Kamadeva, and delighted in watching the arrows of love strike home. No doubt I made it more enjoyable for him. Because I could not hide my feelings. Soon Dinesh would know, too—and then?

A year ago my feelings about you were almost paternal! Or so I thought... But you are no longer a child and I am a little older too. For when, the night after the picnic, you took my hand and held it against your soft warm cheek, it was the first time that a girl had responded to me so readily, so tenderly. Perhaps it was just innocence but that one action of yours, that acceptance of me, immediately devastated my heart.

Gently, fervently, I kissed your eyes and forehead, your small round mouth, and the lobes of your ears, and your long smooth throat; and I whispered, 'Sushila, I love you, I love you, I love you,' in the same way that millions and millions of love-smitten young men have whispered since time immemorial. What else can one say? I love you, I love you. There is nothing simpler; nothing that can be made to mean any more than that. And what else did I say? That I would look after you and work for you and make you happy; and that too had been said before, and I was in no way different from anyone. I was a man and yet I was a boy again.

We visited the stream again, a day or two later, early in the morning. Using the rocks as stepping stones, we wandered downstream for about a furlong until we reached a pool and a small waterfall and a cool dark cave. The rocks were mostly grey but some were yellow with age and some were cushioned with moss. A forktail stood on a boulder in the middle of the stream, uttering its low pleasant call. Water came dripping down from the sides of the cave, while sunlight filtered through a crevice in the rock ceiling, dappling your face. A spray of water was caught by a shaft of sunlight and at intervals it reflected the colours of the rainbow.

'It is a beautiful place,' you said.

'Come, then,' I said, 'let us bathe.'

Sunil and I removed our clothes and jumped into the pool while you sat down in the shade of a walnut tree and watched us disport ourselves in the water. Like a frog, Sunil leapt and twisted about in the clear, icy water; his eyes shone, his teeth glistened white, his body glowed with sunshine, youth, and the jewels made by drops of water glistening in the sun.

Then we stretched ourselves out beside you and allowed the sun to sink deep into our bodies.

Your feet, laved with dew, stood firm on the quickening grass. There was a butterfly between us: its wings red and gold and heavy with dew. It could not move because of the weight of moisture. And as your foot came nearer and I saw that you would crush it, I said, 'Wait. Don't crush the butterfly, Sushila. It has only a few days in the sun and we have many.'

'And if I spare it,' you said, laughing, 'what will you do for me, what will you pay?'

'Why, anything you say.'

'And will you kiss my foot?'

'Both feet,' I said and did so willingly. For they were no less than the wings of butterflies.

Later, when you ventured near the water, I dragged you in with me. You cried out, not in alarm but with the shock of the cold water, and then, wrenching yourself from my arms, clambered on to the rocks, your thin dress clinging to your thighs, your feet making long patterns on the smooth stone.

Though we tired ourselves out that day, we did not sleep at night. We lay together, you and Sunil on either side of me. Your head rested on my shoulders, your hair lay pressed against my cheek. Sunil had curled himself up into a ball but he was far from being asleep. He took my hand, and he took yours, and he placed them together. And I kissed the tender inside of your hand.

I whispered to you, 'Sushila, there has never been anyone I've loved so much. I've been waiting all these years to find you. For a long time I did not even like women. But you are so different. You care for me, don't you?'

You nodded in the darkness. I could see the outline of your

face in the faint moonlight that filtered through the skylight. You never replied directly to a question. I suppose that was a feminine quality; coyness, perhaps.

'Do you love me, Sushila?'

No answer.

'Not now. When you are a little older. In a year or two.'

Did you nod in the darkness or did I imagine it?

'I know it's too early,' I continued. 'You are still too young. You are still at school. But already you are much wiser than me. I am finding it too difficult to control myself, but I will, since you wish it so. I'm very impatient, I know that, but I'll wait for as long as you make me—two or three or a hundred years. Yes, Sushila, a hundred years!'

Ah, what a pretty speech I made! Romeo could have used some of it; Majnu, too.

And your answer? Just a nod, a little pressure on my hand. I took your fingers and kissed them one by one. Long fingers, as long as mine.

After some time I became aware of Sunil nudging me.

'You are not talking to me,' he complained. 'You are only talking to her. You only love her.'

'I'm terribly sorry. I love you too, Sunil.'

Content with this assurance, he fell asleep; but towards morning, thinking himself in the middle of the bed, he rolled over and landed with a thump on the floor. He didn't know how it had happened and accused me of pushing him out.

'I know you don't want me in the bed,' he said.

It was a good thing Dinesh, in the next room, didn't wake up.

◆

'Have you done any work this week?' asked Dinesh with a look of reproach.

'Not much,' I said.

'You are hardly ever in the house. You are never at your desk. Something seems to have happened to you.'

'I have given myself a holiday, that's all. Can't writers take holidays too?'

'No. You have said so yourself. And anyway, you seem to have taken a permanent holiday.'

'Have you finished that painting of the Tibetan woman?' I asked, trying to change the subject.

'That's the third time you've asked me that question, even though you saw the completed painting a week ago. You're getting very absentminded.'

There was a letter from your old boyfriend; I mean your young boyfriend. It was addressed to Sunil, but I recognized the sender's name and knew it was really for you.

I assumed a look of calm detachment and handed the letter to you. But both you and Sunil sensed my dismay. At first you teased me and showed me the boy's photograph, which had been enclosed (he was certainly good looking in a flashy way); then, finding that I became gloomier every minute, you tried to make amends, assuring me that the correspondence was one-sided and that you no longer replied to his letters.

And that night, to show me that you really cared, you gave me your hand as soon as the lights were out. Sunil was fast asleep.

We sat together at the foot of your bed. I kept my arm about you, while you rested your head against my chest. Your feet lay in repose upon mine. I kept kissing you. And when we lay down together, I loosened your blouse and kissed your small firm breasts, and put my lips to your nipples and felt them grow hard against my mouth.

The shy responsiveness of your kisses soon turned to passion. You clung to me. We had forgotten time and place and circumstance. The light of your eyes had been drowned in that lost look of a woman who desires. For a space we both struggled against desire. Suddenly I had become afraid of myself—afraid for you. I tried to free myself from your clasping arms. But you cried in a low voice, 'Love me! Love me! I want you to love me.'

Another night you fell asleep with your face in the crook of my arm, and I lay awake a long time, conscious of your breathing, of the touch of your hair on my cheek, of the soft warm soles of your feet, of your slim waist and legs.

And in the morning, when the sunshine filled the room, I watched you while you slept—your slim body in repose, your face tranquil, your thin dark hands like sleeping butterflies and then, when you woke, the beautiful untidiness of your hair and the drowsiness in your eyes. You lay folded up like a kitten, your limbs as untouched by self-consciousness as the limbs of a young and growing tree. And during the warmth of the day a bead of sweat rested on your brow like a small pearl.

I tried to remember what you looked like as a child. Even then, I had always been aware of your presence. You must have been nine or ten when I first saw you—thin, dark, plain-faced, always wearing the faded green skirt that was your school uniform. You went about barefoot. Once, when the monsoon arrived, you ran out into the rain with the other children, naked, exulting in the swish of the cool rain. I remembered your beautiful straight legs and thighs, your swift smile, your dark eyes. You say you do not remember playing naked in the rain but that is because you did not see yourself.

I did not notice you growing. Your face did not change very much. You must have been thirteen when you gave up skirts and started wearing the salwar kameez. You had few clothes but the plainness of your dress only seemed to bring out your own radiance. And as you grew older, your eyes became more expressive, your hair longer and glossier, your gestures more graceful. And then, when you came to me in the hills, I found that you had been transformed into a fairy princess of devastating charm.

We were idling away the afternoon on our beds and you were reclining in my arms when Dinesh came in unexpectedly. He said nothing, merely passed through the room and entered his studio. Sunil got a fright and you were momentarily confused. Then you said, 'He knows already,' and I said, 'Yes, he must know.'

Later I spoke to Dinesh. I told him that I wanted to marry you; that I knew I would have to wait until you were older and had finished school—probably two or three years—and that I was prepared to wait although I knew it would be a long and difficult business. I asked him to help me.

He was upset at first, probably because he felt I had been deceptive (which was true), and also because of his own responsibility in the matter. You were his niece and I had made love to you while he had been preoccupied with other things. But after a little while, when he saw that I was sincere and rather confused, he relented.

'It has happened too soon,' he said. 'She is too young for all this. Have you told her that you love her?'

'Of course. Many times.'

'You're a fool, then. Have you told her that you want to marry her?'

'Yes.'

'Fool again. That's not the way it is done. Haven't you lived in India long enough to know that?'

'But I love her.'

'Does she love you?'

'I think so.'

'You think so. Desire isn't love, you must know that. Still, I suppose she does love you, otherwise she would not be holding hands with you all day. But you are quite mad, falling in love with a girl half your age.'

'Well, I'm not exactly an old man. I'm thirty.'

'And she's a schoolgirl.'

'She isn't a girl any more, she's too responsive.'

'Oh, you've found that out, have you?'

'Well...' I said, covered in confusion. 'Well, she has shown that she cares a little. You know that it's years since I took any interest in a girl. You called it unnatural on my part, remember? Well, they simply did not exist for me, that's true.'

'Delayed adolescence,' muttered Dinesh.

'But Sushila is different. She puts me at ease. She doesn't turn away from me. I love her and I want to look after her. I can only do that by marrying her.'

'All right, but take it easy. Don't get carried away. And don't, for God's sake, give her a baby. Not while she's still at school! I will do what I can to help you. But you will have to be patient. And no one else must know of this or I will be blamed for everything. As it is Sunil knows too much, and he's too small to know so much.'

'Oh, he won't tell anyone.'

'I wish you had fallen in love with her two years from now. You will have to wait that long, anyway. Getting married isn't a simple matter. People will wonder why we are in such a hurry, marrying her off as soon as she leaves school. They'll think the worst!'

'Well, people do marry for love you know, even in India. It's happening all the time.'

'But it doesn't happen in our family. You know how orthodox most of them are. They wouldn't appreciate your outlook. You may marry Sushila for love but it will have to *look* like an arranged marriage!'

Little things went wrong that evening.

First, a youth on the road passed a remark which you resented;

and you, most unladylike, but most Punjabi-like, picked up a stone and threw it at him. It struck him on the leg. He was too surprised to say anything and limped off. I remonstrated with you, told you that throwing stones at people often resulted in a fight, then realized that you had probably wanted to see me fighting on your behalf.

Later you were annoyed because I said you were a little absentminded. Then Sunil sulked because I spoke roughly to him (I can't remember why), and refused to talk to me for three hours, which was a record. I kept apologizing but neither of you would listen.

It was all part of a game. When I gave up trying and turned instead to my typewriter and my unfinished story, you came and sat beside me and started playing with my hair. You were jealous of my story, of the fact that it was possible for me to withdraw into my work. And I reflected that a woman had to be jealous of something. If there wasn't another woman, then it was a man's work, or his hobby, or his best friend, or his favourite sweater, or his pet mongoose that made her resentful. There is a story in Kipling about a woman who grew insanely jealous of a horse's saddle because her husband spent an hour every day polishing it with great care and loving kindness.

Would it be like that in marriage, I wondered—an eternal triangle: you, me and the typewriter?

But there were only a few days left before you returned to the plains, so I gladly pushed away the typewriter and took you in my arms instead. After all, once you had gone away, it would be a long, long time before I could hold you in my arms again. I might visit you in Delhi but we would not be able to enjoy the same freedom and intimacy. And while I savoured the salt kiss of your lips, I wondered how long I would have to wait until I could really call you my own.

Dinesh was at college and Sunil had gone roller skating and

we were alone all morning. At first you avoided me, so I picked up a book and pretended to read. But barely five minutes had passed before you stole up from behind and snapped the book shut.

'It is a warm day,' you said. 'Let us go down to the stream.'

Alone together for the first time, we took the steep path down to the stream, and there, hand in hand, scrambled over the rocks until we reached the pool and the waterfall.

I will bathe today,' you said, and in a few moments you stood beside me, naked, caressed by sunlight and a soft breeze coming down the valley. I put my hand out to share in the sun's caress, but you darted away, laughing, and ran to the waterfall as though you would hide behind a curtain of gushing water. I was soon beside you. I took you in my arms and kissed you, while the water crashed down upon our heads. Who yielded—you or I? All I remember is that you had entwined yourself about me like a clinging vine, and that a little later we lay together on the grass, on bruised and broken clover, while a whistling thrush released its deep sweet secret on the trembling air.

Blackbird on the wing, bird of the forest shadows, black rose in the long ago of summer, this was your song. It isn't time that's passing by, it is you and I.

It was your last night under my roof. We were not alone but when I woke in the middle of the night and stretched my hand out, across the space between our beds, you took my hand, for you were awake too. Then I pressed the ends of your fingers, one by one, as I had done so often before, and you dug your nails into my flesh. And our hands made love, much as our bodies might have done. They clung together, warmed and caressed each other, each finger taking on an identity of its own and seeking its opposite. Sometimes the tips of our fingers merely brushed against each other, teasingly, and sometimes our palms met with a rush, would tremble and embrace, separate, and then passionately seek each other out. And when sleep finally overcame you, your hand fell listlessly between our beds, touching the ground. And I lifted it up, and after putting it once to my lips, returned it gently to your softly rising bosom.

And so you went away, all three of you, and I was left alone with the brooding mountain. If I could not pass a few weeks without you, how was I to pass a year, two years? This was the question I kept asking myself. Would I have to leave the hills and take a flat in Delhi? And what use would it be—looking at you and speaking to you but never able to touch you? Not to be able to touch that which I had already possessed would have been the subtlest form of torture.

The house was empty but I kept finding little things to remind me that you had been there—a handkerchief, a bangle, a length of ribbon—and these remnants made me feel as though you had gone forever. No sound at night, except the rats scurrying about on the rafters.

The rain had brought out the ferns, which were springing up from tree and rock. The murmur of the stream had become an angry rumble. The honeysuckle creeper winding over the front windows was thick with scented blossom. I wish it had flowered a little earlier, before you left. Then you could have put the flowers in your hair.

At night I drank brandy, wrote listlessly, listened to the wind in the chimney and read poetry in bed. There was no one to tell stories to and no hand to hold.

I kept remembering little things—the soft hair hiding your ears, the movement of your hands, the cool touch of your feet, the tender look in your eyes and the sudden stab of mischief that sometimes replaced it.

Mrs Kapoor remarked on the softness of your expression. I was glad that someone had noticed it. In my diary I wrote:

'I have looked at Sushila so often and so much that perhaps I have overlooked her most compelling qualities—her kindness (or is it just her easygoingness?), her refusal to hurt anyone's feelings (or is it just her indifference to everything?), her wide tolerance (or is it just her laziness?)... Oh, how absolutely ignorant I am of women!'

Well, there was a letter from Dinesh and it held out a lifeline, one that I knew I must seize without any hesitation. He said he might be joining an art school in Delhi and asked me if I would like to return to Delhi and share a flat with him. I had always dreaded the possibility of leaving the hills and living again in a city as depressing as Delhi but love, I considered, ought to make any place habitable...

And then I was on a bus on the road to Delhi.

The first monsoon showers had freshened the fields and everything looked much greener than usual. The maize was just shooting up and the mangoes were ripening fast. Near the larger villages, camels and bullock carts cluttered up the road, and the driver cursed, banging his fist on the horn.

Passing through small towns, the bus driver had to contend with cycle rickshaws, tonga ponies, trucks, pedestrians and other buses. Coming down from the hills for the first time in over a year, I found the noise, chaos, dust and dirt a little unsettling.

As my taxi drew up at the gate of Dinesh's home, Sunil saw me and came running to open the car door. Other children were soon swarming around me. Then I saw you standing near the front door. You raised your hand to your forehead in a typical Muslim form of greeting—a gesture you had picked up, I suppose, from a film.

For two days Dinesh and I went house hunting, for I had decided to take a flat if it was at all practicable. Either it was very hot, and we were sweating, or it was raining and we were drenched. (It is difficult to find a flat in Delhi, even if one is in a position to pay an exorbitant rent, which I was not. It is especially difficult for bachelors. No one trusts bachelors, especially if there are grown-up daughters in the house. Is this because bachelors are wolves or because girls are so easily seduced these days?)

Finally, after several refusals, we were offered a flat in one of those new colonies that sprout like mushrooms around the capital. The rent was two hundred rupees a month and although I knew I couldn't really afford so much, I was so sick of refusals and already so disheartened and depressed that I took the place and made out a cheque to the landlord, an elderly gentleman with his daughters all safely married in other parts of the country.

There was no furniture in the flat except for a couple of beds, but we decided we would fill the place up gradually. Everyone at Dinesh's home—brothers, sister-in-law, aunts, nephews and nieces—helped us to move in. Sunil and his younger brother were the first arrivals. Later the other children, some ten of them, arrived. You, Sushila, came only in the afternoon, but I had gone out for something and only saw you when I returned at tea time. You were sitting on the first-floor balcony and smiled down at me as I walked up the road.

I think you were pleased with the flat; or at any rate, with my courage in taking one. I took you up to the roof, and there, in a corner under the stairs, kissed you very quickly. It had to be quick, because the other children were close on our heels. There wouldn't be much opportunity for kissing you again. The mountains were far and in a place like Delhi, and with a family like yours, private moments would be few and far between.

Hours later when I sat alone on one of the beds, Sunil came to me, looking rather upset. He must have had a quarrel with you.

'I want to tell you something,' he said.

'Is anything wrong?'

To my amazement he burst into tears.

'Now you must not love me anymore,' he said.

'Why not?'

'Because you are going to marry Sushila, and if you love me too much it will not be good for you.'

I could think of nothing to say. It was all too funny and all too sad.

But a little later he was in high spirits, having apparently forgotten the reasons for his earlier dejection. His need for affection stemmed perhaps from his father's long and unnecessary absence from the country.

Dinesh and I had no sleep during our first night in the new flat. We were near the main road and traffic roared past all night. I thought of the hills, so silent that the call of a nightjar startled one in the stillness of the night.

I was out most of the next day and when I got back in the evening it was to find that Dinesh had had a rumpus with the landlord. Apparently the landlord had really wanted bachelors, and couldn't understand or appreciate a large number of children moving in and out of the house all day.

'I thought landlords preferred having families,' I said.

'He wants to know how a bachelor came to have such a large family!'

'Didn't you tell him that the children were only temporary, and wouldn't be living here?'

'I did, but he doesn't believe me.'

'Well, anyway, we're not going to stop the children from coming to see us,' I said indignantly. (No children, no Sushila!) 'If he doesn't see reason, he can have his flat back.'

'Did he cash my cheque?'

'No, he's given it back.'

'That means he really wants us out. To hell with his flat! It's too noisy here anyway. Let's go back to your place.'

We packed our bedding, trunks and kitchen utensils once more;

hired a bullock cart and arrived at Dinesh's home (three miles distant) late at night, hungry and upset.

Everything seemed to be going wrong.

Living in the same house as you, but unable to have any real contact with you (except for the odd, rare moment when we were left alone in the same room and were able to exchange a word or a glance) was an exquisite form of self-inflicted torture: self-inflicted, because no one was forcing me to stay in Delhi. Sometimes you had to avoid me and I could not stand that. Only Dinesh (and, of course, Sunil and some of the children) knew anything about the affair—adults are much slower than children at sensing the truth—and it was still too soon to reveal the true state of affairs and my own feelings to anyone else in the family. If I came out with the declaration that I was in love with you, it would immediately become obvious that something had happened during your holiday in the hill station. It would be said that I had taken advantage of the situation (which I had), and that I had seduced you—even though I was beginning to wonder if it was you who had seduced me! And if a marriage was suddenly arranged, people would say: 'It's been arranged so quickly. And she's so young. He must have got her into trouble.' Even though there were no signs of your having got into that sort of trouble.

And yet I could not help hoping that you would become my wife sooner than could be foreseen. I wanted to look after you. I did not want others to be doing it for me. Was that very selfish? Or was it a true state of being in love?

There were times—times when you kept your distance and did not even look at me—when I grew desperate. I knew you could not show your familiarity with me in front of others and yet, knowing this, I still tried to catch your eye, to sit near you, to touch you fleetingly. I could not hold myself back. I became morose, I wallowed in self-pity. And self-pity, I realized, is a sign of failure, especially of failure in love.

It was time to return to the hills.

Sushila, when I got up in the morning to leave, you were still asleep and I did not wake you. I watched you stretched out on your bed, your dark face tranquil and untouched by care, your black hair spread over the white pillow, your long thin hands and feet in repose. You were so beautiful when you were asleep.

And as I watched, I felt a tightening around my heart, a sudden panic that I might somehow lose you.

The others were up and there was no time to steal a kiss. A taxi was at the gate. A baby was bawling. Your grandmother was giving me advice. The taxi driver kept blowing his horn.

Goodbye, Sushila!

We were in the middle of the rains. There was a constant drip and drizzle and drumming on the corrugated tin roof. The walls were damp and there was mildew on my books and even on the pickle that Dinesh had made.

Everything was green, the foliage almost tropical, especially near the stream. Great stag ferns grew from the trunks of trees, fresh moss covered the rocks, and the maidenhair fern was at its loveliest. The water was a torrent, rushing through the ravine and taking with it bushes and small trees. I could not remain out for long, for at any moment it might start raining. And there were also the leeches who lost no time in fastening themselves on to my legs and feasting on my blood.

Once, standing on some rocks, I saw a slim brown snake swimming with the current. It looked beautiful and lonely. I dreamt a dream, very disturbing dream, which troubled me for days.

In the dream, Sunil suggested that we go down to the stream. We put some bread and butter into an airbag, along with a long bread knife, and set off down the hill. Sushila was barefoot, wearing the old cotton tunic which she had worn as a child; Sunil had on a bright yellow T-shirt and black jeans. He looked very dashing. As we took the forest path down to the stream, we saw two young men following us. One of them, a dark, slim youth, seemed familiar. I said, 'Isn't that Sushila's boyfriend?' But they denied it. The other youth wasn't anyone I knew.

When we reached the stream, Sunil and I plunged into the pool, while Sushila sat on the rock just above us. We had been bathing for a few minutes when the two young men came down the slope and began fondling Sushila. She did not resist but Sunil climbed out of the pool and began scrambling up the slope. One of the youths, the less familiar one, had a long knife in his hand. Sunil picked up a stone and flung it at the youth, striking him on the shoulder. I rushed up and grabbed the hand that held the knife. The youth kicked me on the shins and thrust me away and I fell beneath him. The arm with the knife was raised over me, but I still held the wrist. And then I saw Sushila behind him, her face framed by a passing cloud. She had the bread knife in her hand, and her arm swung up and down, and the knife cut through my adversary's neck as though it were passing through a ripe melon.

I scrambled to my feet to find Sushila gazing at the headless corpse with the detachment and mild curiosity of a child who has just removed the wings from a butterfly. The other youth, who looked like Sushila's boyfriend, began running away. He was chased by the three of us. When he slipped and fell, I found myself beside him, the blade of the knife poised beneath his left shoulder blade. I couldn't push the knife in. Then Sunil put his hand over mine and the blade slipped smoothly into the flesh.

At all times of the day and night I could hear the murmur of the stream at the bottom of the hill. Even if I didn't listen, the sound was there. I had grown used to it. But whenever I went away, I was conscious of something missing and I was lonely without the sound of running water.

I remained alone for two months and then I had to see you again, Sushila. I could not bear the long-drawn-out uncertainty of the situation. I wanted to do something that would bring everything nearer to a conclusion. Merely to stand by and wait was intolerable. Nor could I bear the secrecy to which Dinesh had sworn me. Someone else would have to know about my intentions—someone would have to help. I needed another ally to sustain my hopes; only then would I find the waiting easier.

You had not been keeping well and looked thin, but you were as cheerful, as serene as ever.

When I took you to the pictures with Sunil, you wore a sleeveless kameez made of purple silk. It set off your dark beauty very well. Your face was soft and shy and your smile hadn't changed. I could not keep my eyes off you.

Returning home in the taxi, I held your hand all the way.

Sunil (in Punjabi): 'Will you give your children English or Hindi names?'

Me: 'Hindustani names.'

Sunil (in Punjabi): 'Ah, that is the right answer, Uncle!'

And first I went to your mother.

She was a tiny woman and looked very delicate. But she'd had six children—a seventh was on the way—and they had all come into the world without much difficulty and were the healthiest in the entire joint family.

She was on her way to see relatives in another part of the city and I accompanied her part of the way. As she was pregnant, she was offered a seat in the crowded bus. I managed to squeeze in beside her. She had always shown a liking for me and I did not find it difficult to come to the point.

'At what age would you like Sushila to get married?' I asked casually, with almost paternal interest.

'We'll worry about that when the time comes. She has still

to finish school. And if she keeps failing her exams, she will never finish school.'

I took a deep breath and made the plunge.

'When the time comes,' I said, 'when the time comes, I would like to marry her.' And without waiting to see what her reaction would be, I continued: 'I know I must wait a year or two, even longer. But I am telling you this, so that it will be in your mind. You are her mother and so I want you to be the first to know.' (Liar that I was! She was about the fifth to know. But what I really wanted to say was, 'Please don't be looking for any other husband for her just yet.')

She didn't show much surprise. She was a placid woman. But she said, rather sadly, 'It's all right but I don't have much say in the family. I do not have any money, you see. It depends on the others, especially her grandmother.'

'I'll speak to them when the time comes. Don't worry about that. And you don't have to worry about money or anything—what I mean is, I don't believe in dowries—I mean, you don't have to give me a Godrej cupboard and a sofa set and that sort of thing. All I want is Sushila…'

'She is still very young.'

But she was pleased—pleased that her flesh and blood, her own daughter, could mean so much to a man.

'Don't tell anyone else just now,' I said.

'I won't tell anyone,' she said with a smile.

So now the secret—if it could be called that—was shared by at least five people.

The bus crawled on through the busy streets and we sat in silence, surrounded by a press of people but isolated in the intimacy of our conversation.

I warmed towards her—towards that simple, straightforward, uneducated woman (she had never been to school, could not read or write), who might still have been young and pretty had her circumstances been different. I asked her when the baby was due.

'In two months,' she said. She laughed. Evidently she found it unusual and rather amusing for a young man to ask her such a question.

'I'm sure it will be a fine baby,' I said. And I thought: That makes six brothers-in-law!

I did not think I would get a chance to speak to your Uncle Ravi (Dinesh's elder brother) before I left. But on my last evening in Delhi, I found myself alone with him on the Karol Bagh road. At first we spoke of his own plans for marriage, and, to please him, I said the girl he'd chosen was both beautiful and intelligent.

He warmed towards me.

Clearing my throat, I went on. 'Ravi, you are five years younger than me and you are about to get married.'

'Yes, and it's time you thought of doing the same thing.'

'Well, I've never thought seriously about it before—I'd always scorned the institution of marriage—but now I've changed my mind. Do you know whom I'd like to marry?'

To my surprise Ravi unhesitatingly took the name of Asha, a distant cousin I'd met only once. She came from Ferozepur, and her hips were so large that from a distance she looked like an oversized pear.

'No, no,' I said. 'Asha is a lovely girl but I wasn't thinking of her. I would like to marry a girl like Sushila. To be frank, Ravi, I would like to marry Sushila.'

There was a long silence and I feared the worst. The noise of cars, scooters and buses seemed to recede into the distance and Ravi and I were alone together in a vacuum of silence.

So that the awkwardness would not last too long, I stumbled on with what I had to say. 'I know she's young and that I will have to wait for some time.' (Familiar words!) 'But if you approve, and the family approves, and Sushila approves, well then, there's nothing I'd like better than to marry her.'

Ravi pondered, scratched himself, and then, to my delight, said: 'Why not? It's a fine idea.'

The traffic sounds returned to the street, and I felt as though I could set fire to a bus or do something equally in keeping with my high spirits.

'It would bring you even closer to us,' said Ravi. 'We would like to have you in our family. At least I would like it.'

'That makes all the difference,' I said. 'I will do my best for her, Ravi. I'll do everything to make her happy.'

'She is very simple and unspoilt.'

'I know. That's why I care so much for her.'

'I will do what I can to help you. She should finish school by the time she is seventeen. It does not matter if you are older. Twelve years difference in age is not uncommon. So don't worry. Be patient and all will be arranged.'

And so I had three strong allies—Dinesh, Ravi and your mother. Only your grandmother remained, and I dared not approach her on my own. She was the most difficult hurdle because she was the head of the family and she was autocratic and often unpredictable. She was not on good terms with your mother and for that very reason I feared that she might oppose my proposal. I had no idea how much she valued Ravi's and Dinesh's judgement. All I knew was that they bowed to all her decisions.

How impossible it was for you to shed the burden of your relatives! Individually, you got on quite well with all of them; but because they could not live without bickering among themselves, you were just a pawn in the great joint family game.

You put my hand to your cheek and to your breast. I kissed your closed eyes and took your face in my hands, and touched your lips with mine; a phantom kiss in the darkness of a verandah.

And then, intoxicated, I stumbled into the road and walked the streets all night.

I was sitting on the rocks above the oak forest when I saw a young man walking towards me down the steep path. From his careful manner of walking, and light clothing, I could tell that he was a stranger, one who was not used to the hills. He was about my height, slim, rather long in the face; good looking in a delicate sort of way. When he came nearer, I recognized him as the young man in the photograph, the youth of my dream—your late admirer! I wasn't too surprised to see him. Somehow, I had always felt that we would meet one day.

I remembered his name and said, 'How are you, Pramod?'

He became rather confused. His eyes were already clouded with doubt and unhappiness; but he did not appear to be an aggressive person.

'How did you know my name?' he asked.

'How did you know where to find me?' I countered.

'Your neighbours, the Kapoors, told me. I could not wait for you to return to the house. I have to go down again tonight.'

'Well then, would you like to walk home with me, or would you prefer to sit here and talk? I know who you are but I've no idea why you've come to see me.'

'It's all right here,' he said, spreading his handkerchief on the grass before sitting down on it. 'How did you know my name?'

I stared at him for a few moments and got the impression that he was a vulnerable person—perhaps more vulnerable than myself.

My only advantage was that I was older and therefore better able to conceal my real feelings.

'Sushila told me,' I said.

'Oh. I did not think you would know.'

I was a little puzzled but said, 'I knew about you, of course. And you must have known that or you would hardly have come here to see me.'

'You knew about Sushila and me?' he asked, looking even more confused.

'Well, I know that you are supposed to be in love with her.'

He smote himself on the forehead. 'My God! Do the others know, too?'

'I don't think so.' I deliberately avoided mention of Sunil.

In his distraction he started plucking at tufts of grass. 'Did she tell you?' he asked.

'Yes.'

'Girls can't keep secrets. But in a way I'm glad she told you. Now I don't have to explain everything. You see, I came here for your help. I know you are not her real uncle but you are very close to her family. Last year in Delhi she often spoke about you. She said you were very kind.'

It then occurred to me that Pramod knew nothing about my relationship with you, other than that I was supposed to be the most benevolent of 'uncles'. He knew that you had spent your summer holidays with me—but so had Dinesh and Sunil. And now, aware that I was a close friend of the family, he had come to make an ally of me—in much the same way that I had gone about making allies!

'Have you seen Sushila recently?' I asked.

'Yes. Two days ago, in Delhi. But I had only a few minutes alone with her. We could not talk much. You see, Uncle—you will not mind if I also call you uncle? I want to marry her but there is no one who can speak to her people on my behalf. My own parents are not alive. If I go straight to her family, most probably I will be thrown out of the house. So I want you to help me. I am not well off but I will soon have a job and then I can support her.

'Did you tell her all this?'

'Yes.'

'And what did she say?'

'She told me to speak to you about it.'

Clever Sushila! Diabolical Sushila!

'To me?' I repeated.

'Yes, she said it would be better than talking to her parents.'

I couldn't help laughing. And a long-tailed blue magpie, disturbed by my laughter, set up a shrill creaking and chattering of its own.

'Don't laugh, I'm serious, Uncle,' said Pramod. He took me by the hand and looked at me appealingly.

'Well, it ought to be serious,' I said. 'How old are you, Pramod?'

'Twenty-three.'

'Only seven years younger than me. So please don't call me uncle. It makes me feel prehistoric. Use my first name, if you like. And when do you hope to marry Sushila?'

'As soon as possible. I know she is still very young for me.'

'Not at all,' I said, 'Young girls are marrying middle-aged men every day! And you're still quite young yourself. But she can't get married as yet, Pramod, I know that for a certainty.'

'That's what I feared. She will have to finish school, I suppose.'

'That's right. But tell me something. It's obvious that you are in love with her and I don't blame you for it. Sushila is the kind of girl we all fall in love with! But do you know if she loves you? Did she say she would like to marry you?'

'She did not say—I do not know…'

There was a haunted, hurt look in his eyes and my heart went out to him. 'But I love her—isn't that enough?'

'It could be enough—provided she doesn't love someone else.'

'Does she, Uncle?'

'To be frank, I don't know.'

He brightened up at that. 'She likes me,' he said. 'I know that much.'

'Well, I like you too, but that doesn't mean I'd marry you.'

He was despondent again. 'I see what you mean... But what is love, how can I recognize it?'

And that was one question I couldn't answer. How do we recognize it?

I persuaded Pramod to stay the night. The sun had gone down and he was shivering. I made a fire, the first of the winter, using oak and thorn branches. Then I shared my brandy with him.

I did not feel any resentment against Pramod. Prior to meeting him, I had been jealous. And when I first saw him coming along the path, I remembered my dream, and thought, 'Perhaps I am going to kill him, after all. Or perhaps he's going to kill me.' But it had turned out differently. If dreams have any meaning at all, the meaning doesn't come within our limited comprehension.

I had visualized Pramod as being rather crude, selfish and irresponsible, an unattractive college student, the type who has never known or understood girls very well and looks on them as strange exotic creatures who are to be seized and plundered at the first opportunity. Such men do exist but Pramod was never one of them. He did not know much about women; neither did I. He was gentle, polite, unsure of himself. I wondered if I should tell him about my own feelings for you.

After a while he began to talk about himself and about you. He told me how he fell in love with you. At first he had been friendly with another girl, a classfellow of yours, but a year or two older. You had carried messages to him on the girl's behalf. Then the girl had rejected him. He was terribly depressed and one evening he drank a lot of cheap liquor. Instead of falling dead, as he had been hoping, he lost his way and met you near your home. He was in need of sympathy and you gave him that. You let him hold your hand. He told you how hopeless he felt and you comforted him. And when he said the world was a cruel place, you consented. You agreed with him. What more can a man expect from a woman? Only fourteen at the time, you had no difficulty in comforting a man of twenty-two. No wonder he fell in love with you!

Afterwards you met occasionally on the road and spoke to each other. He visited the house once or twice, on some pretext or other. And when you came to the hills, he wrote to you.

That was all he had to tell me. That was all there was to tell. You had touched his heart once and touching it, had no difficulty in capturing it.

Next morning I took Pramod down to the stream. I wanted to tell him everything and somehow I could not do it in the house.

He was charmed by the place. The water flowed gently, its music subdued, soft chamber music after the monsoon orchestration. Cowbells tinkled on the hillside and an eagle soared high above.

'I did not think water could be so clear,' said Pramod. 'It is not muddy like the streams and rivers of the plains.'

'In the summer you can bathe here,' I said. 'There is a pool further downstream.'

He nodded thoughtfully. 'Did she come here too?'

'Yes, Sushila and Sunil and I... We came here on two or three occasions.' My voice trailed off and I glanced at Pramod standing at the edge of the water. He looked up at me and his eyes met mine.

'There is something I want to tell you,' I said.

He continued staring at me and a shadow seemed to pass across his face—a shadow of doubt, fear, death, eternity, was it one or all of these, or just a play of light and shade? But I remembered my dream and stepped back from him. For a moment, both of us looked at each other with distrust and uncertainty. Then the fear passed. Whatever had happened between us, dream or reality, had happened in some other existence. Now he took my hand and held it, held it tight, as though seeking assurance, as though identifying himself with me.

'Let us sit down,' I said. 'There is something I must tell you.'

We sat down on the grass and when I looked up through the branches of the banj oak, everything seemed to have been tilted and held at an angle, and the sky shocked me with its blueness, and the leaves were no longer green but purple in the shadows of the ravine. They were your colour, Sushila. I remembered you wearing purple—dark, smiling Sushila, thinking your own thoughts and refusing to share them with anyone.

'I love Sushila too,' I said.

'I know,' he said naively. 'That is why I came to you for help.'

'No, you don't know,' I said. 'When I say "I love Sushila", I mean just that. I mean caring for her in the same way that you care for her. I mean I want to marry her.'

'You, Uncle?'

'Yes. Does it shock you very much?'

'No, no.' He turned his face away and stared at the worn face of an old grey rock and perhaps he drew some strength from its permanency. 'Why should you not love her? Perhaps, in my heart, I really knew it, but did not want to know—did not want to believe. Perhaps that is why I really came here—to find out. Something that Sunil said…'

'But why didn't you tell me before?'

'Because you were telling me!'

'Yes, I was too full of my own love to think that any other was possible. What do we do now? Do we both wait and then let her make her choice?'

'If you wish.'

'You have the advantage, Uncle. You have more to offer.'

'Do you mean more security or more love? Some women place more value on the former.'

'Not Sushila.'

'I mean you can offer her a more interesting life. You are a writer. Who knows, you may be famous one day.'

'You have your youth to offer, Pramod. I have only a few years of youth left to me—and two or three of them will pass in waiting.'

'Oh, no,' he said. 'You will always be young. If you have Sushila, you will always be young.'

Once again I heard the whistling thrush. Its song was a crescendo of sweet notes and variations that rang clearly across the ravine. I could not see the bird but its call emerged from the forest like some dark sweet secret and again it was saying, 'It isn't time that's passing by, my friend. It is you and I.'

Listen. Sushila, the worst has happened. Ravi has written to say that a marriage will not be possible—not now, not next year; never. Of course he makes a lot of excuses—that you must receive a complete college education ('higher studies'), that the difference in our age is too great, that you might change your mind after a year or two—but reading between the lines, I can guess that the real reason is your grandmother. She does not want it. Her word is law and no one, least of all Ravi, would dare oppose her. But I do not mean to give in so easily. I will wait my chance. As long as I know that you are with me, I will wait my chance.

I wonder what the old lady objects to in me. Is it simply that she is conservative and tradition-bound? She has always shown a liking for me and I don't see why her liking should change because I want to marry her grandniece. Your mother has no objection.

Perhaps that's why your grandmother objects. Whatever the reason, I am coming down to Delhi to find out how things stand.

Of course the worst part is that Ravi has asked me—in the friendliest terms and in a most roundabout manner—not to come to the house for some time. He says this will give the affair a chance to cool off and die a natural (I would call it an unnatural) death. He assumes, of course, that I will accept the old lady's decision and simply forget all about you. Ravi is yet to fall in love.

Dinesh was in Lucknow. I could not visit the house. So I sat on a bench in the Talkatora Gardens and watched a group of children playing gulli danda. Then I recalled that Sunil's school got over at three o'clock and that if I hurried I would be able to meet him outside the St Columba's gate.

I reached the school on time. Boys were streaming out of the compound and as they were all wearing green uniforms—a young forest on the move—I gave up all hope of spotting Sunil. But he saw me first. He ran across the road, dodged a cyclist, evaded a bus and seized me about the waist.

'I'm so happy to see you, Uncle!'

'As I am to see you, Sunil.'

'You want to see Sushila?'

'Yes, but you too. I can't come to the house, Sunil. You probably know that. When do you have to be home?'

'About four o'clock. If I'm late, I'll say the bus was too crowded and I couldn't get in.'

'That gives us an hour or two. Let's go to the exhibition grounds. Would you like that?'

'All right, I haven't seen the exhibition yet.'

We took a scooter rickshaw to the exhibition grounds on Mathura Road. It was an industrial exhibition and there was little to interest either a schoolboy or a lovesick author. But a cafe was at hand, overlooking an artificial lake, and we sat in the sun, consuming hot dogs and cold coffee.

'Sunil, will you help me?' I asked.

'Whatever you say, Uncle.'

'I don't suppose I can see Sushila this time. I don't want to hang about near the house or her school like a disreputable character. It's all right lurking outside a boys' school; but it wouldn't do to be hanging about the Kanyadevi Pathshala or wherever it is she's studying. It's possible the family will change their minds about us later. Anyway, what matters now is Sushila's attitude. Ask her this, Sunil. Ask her if she wants me to wait until she is eighteen.

'She will be free then to do what she wants, even to run away with me if necessary—that is, if she really wants to. I was ready to wait two years. I'm prepared to wait three. But it will help if I know she's waiting too. Will you ask her that, Sunil?'

'Yes, I'll ask her.'

'Ask her tonight. Then tomorrow we'll meet again outside your school.'

We met briefly the next day. There wasn't much time. Sunil had to be home early and I had to catch the night train out of Delhi. We stood in the generous shade of a peepul tree and I asked,

'What did she say?'

'She said to keep waiting.'

'All right, I'll wait.'

'But when she is eighteen, what if she changes her mind? You know what girls are like.'

'You're a cynical chap, Sunil.'

'What does that mean?'

'It means you know too much about life. But tell me—what makes you think she might change her mind?'

'Her boyfriend.'

'Pramod? She doesn't care for him, poor chap.'

'Not Pramod. Another one.'

'Another! You mean a new one?'

'New,' said Sunil. 'An officer in a bank. He's got a car.'

'Oh,' I said despondently. 'I can't compete with a car.'

'No,' said Sunil. 'Never mind, Uncle. You still have me for your friend. Have you forgotten that?'

I had almost forgotten but it was good to be reminded.

'It is time to go,' he said. 'I must catch the bus today. When will you come to Delhi again?'

'Next month. Next year. Who knows? But I'll come. Look after yourself, my friend.'

He ran off and jumped on to the footboard of a moving bus. He waved to me until the bus went round the bend in the road.

It was lonely under the peepul tree. It is said that only ghosts live in peepul trees. I do not blame them, for peepul trees are cool and shady and full of loneliness.

I may stop loving you, Sushila, but I will never stop loving the days I loved you.